A Groom for Heather

THE BLIZZARD BRIDES #13

Christine Sterling

A GROOM FOR HEATHER

A Groom for Heather ©2021 Christine Sterling
Cover Design by Erin Dameron-Hill Graphics
https://www.edhprofessionals.com/
Editing by Carolyn Leggo and Amy Petrowich

www.christinesterling.com
1st Ed, 4/2021

TABLE OF CONTENTS

A GROOM FOR HEATHER

When Heather Barnes loses her beloved husband to the terrible blizzard that claimed so many lives, she must decide where her future lies. It was her husband who led all the men to their fate, and now she feels responsible that the women must remarry so quickly. The last thing she wants is another husband, but taking care of the farm, hunting, the butcher shop, and being a mother to two orphan children, is too much for the woman that is also the town's midwife. What she doesn't count on is a traveling gunslinger making her question her choice to love again.

Dalton James left everything behind to chase after his brother's killer. Five years on the frontier have roughened him into a man that legends are made from. Now, instead of chasing outlaws, he envisions a life where revenge and traveling are no longer necessary. He didn't count on finding his future so quickly in the form of a blue-eyed lady doctor. When the object of his affection has decided she isn't going to marry any man, can Dalton convince her to stay and take a chance on a new future with him?

What happens when a secret Dalton has been hiding comes to light, putting his love and the women of Last Chance in danger? Will Last Chance become a second chance at love for Dalton and Heather?

LICENSE NOTE

GET FREE BOOKS

Join the Chat, Sip & Read newsletter to stay updated with new releases, access to exclusive bonus content, and more!

Join the CSR newsletter here:

www.chatsipandread.com

CHAPTER ONE

November 1878, New Mexico Territory, along the southern border

Dalton James looked at the body on the travois. The scent of blood and decay filled his nostrils, forcing him to take a step back. Not even the spruce branches someone laid around the body could cover the scent of death.

Five long years were ending as Dalton gazed on the deceased body of Frank Drummond. His skin was mottled in black, blue, and red. It was almost as if someone had beat the man to death.

Too bad it wasn't me that did the deed, Dalton thought. He watched as the Marshal placed two pennies on Frank's eyes to keep them closed.

"Yeah," he said turning away. "That's him. How

did it happen?"

The marshal looked at Dalton and moved his cigarillo to the corner of his mouth with tar-colored fingers. "Mule."

"Mule?" Dalton scratched his chin. He hadn't shaved in nearly a year. He needed to find a bathhouse once he dealt with the matter at hand. "You sure?"

"Yep. I guess he snuck in the barn where Widow Hendricks had her mule. Sally don't take kindly to strangers. Took several days before she found him; the stench gave it away."

"It took her several days to realize there was a dead man in her barn?"

The marshal inhaled deeply and blew the bitter smoke tinged with cherry wood in the air. "She's a peculiar sort."

"Widow Hendricks or the mule?"

The marshal chuckled. "I guess both. He mustava crawled to the back of the barn and died in some hay. She don't go in there too often. The animals normally let themselves out."

Dalton shook his head. He didn't want to ask any more questions about the widow, or her animals. He released a heavy sigh and scrubbed his hand down his face. Disappointment coursed through his body. This wasn't the way he expected it to end.

"Thanks, Marshal," Dalton said reaching out to

shake the marshal's hand. "I appreciate you finding me."

"It just so happened that several men knew you were in town, so I was able to find you. Your reputation precedes you. If'un you don't mind me asking, what was your business with Drummond?"

Dalton took a deep swallow and gazed out at the Colorado landscape. "He killed my brother," he finally said. "I wanted to kill him myself."

"How long you been looking for him?"

Dalton watched as a large black bird flew in circles, hovering on the gusts of wind.

Closing his eyes, he exhaled. "Five long years."

"That's a long time to chase someone."

Dalton opened his eyes and looked at the weathered marshal. "I'm afraid I wasn't very good at it."

The marshal spat on the ground. Dalton wrinkled his nose. His mother taught the boys that smoking was a horrible habit, and she pressed that point home when she caught Dalton and his brother smoking in the hayloft. Neither could sit for a week after that. He recalled that the barn a few miles down the road from where they grew up went up in flames from a cowboy sneaking a smoke inside.

Those were the type of impressions that stayed with him.

"Well, you don't have to worry about him now." Dalton nodded. "You headed home?"

"Not sure. I think I'll stay for a few more days and then head out. I've spent so long trying to figure out Drummond's next steps that I don't know what's next."

"Stop by and see me before you head out of town."

"Any reason in particular?"

"Just want to know you are leaving. That way no one gets any ideas of trying to goad you into a gunfight."

Dalton headed back across the street and lifted his hand towards the marshal. "Will do," he said.

He wanted to go back to the hotel, but he had a few pieces of business to tend to. Walking to the telegraph office he sent a note to his mother back home in Ohio and then headed towards the mercantile. When he caught a glance at his reflection he grimaced. He looked more like a mountain man than a man from the Ohio Valley.

Entering the mercantile he walked straight to the display with men's linen shirts and wool pants.

"Can I help you?" a haughty voice asked.

Dalton turned and looked at a woman who was no higher than a grasshopper staring back at him. Her graying hair was in such a tight topknot that it looked as though her eyes were trying to touch the corners of her head. She peered at him over the rim of her spectacles, distrust evident on her face.

"I'm just looking," he responded.

"Don't touch the merchandise," she said, adjusting the shirt on the tailor's dummy next to the table. She peered at him once more. "And we don't extend credit."

Dalton smiled. "Yes ma'am." He reached into his pocket and pulled out several bills. "I'll be paying cash. I just need a clean shirt, pants, and some boots."

The woman squinted her eyes. Reaching out, she snatched the bills in Dalton's hands, and with a flick of her thumb, started counting them. "That will be more than enough to get you outfitted."

"Yes, ma'am. I also need to know where the bathhouse is."

The woman stopped and handed the bills back to Dalton. "You can get a bath at the saloon."

Dalton flinched. He had no desire to go back to a saloon. He closed his eyes and took a deep breath before opening them once more. "Thank you," he said. He wondered how much it would cost for a bath at the hotel. It was probably three times the price.

The woman took a shirt from the stack on the table. "This should fit you," she said. Shaking out a pair of woolen pants, she held them up to Dalton before putting them back on the table and taking another.

"These will do." She picked up both the shirt and pants and carried them to the front counter. "You said you needed shoes?"

"Boots."

"What kind do you want?"

Dalton shrugged. "Preferably ones without holes."

The woman pulled out a pair of black Congress Gaiters and held them out. "All the way from New York City. You won't find a more comfortable pair of boots anywhere."

Dalton took one out of the woman's hand and looked at it. The boot was crafted of black leather with a small heel and a decorative trim over the front. Laces threaded through eyelets to secure the boot to a person's foot. The leather rose to just above the ankle. "How much are they?"

"Ten dollars."

"Ten dollars?" Dalton nearly dropped the boot. He handed it back to the woman. "I just want a pair of plain stovetop-style boots. Those look like dandy boots."

The woman frowned and put the boots back on the shelf. Given that there were several pairs gathering dust, Dalton surmised that they weren't one of the mercantile's best sellers. He reached over and picked up a pair of boots he had seen the stockmen wear in town. They were crafted of dark brown leather with square toes and stacked heels. The stovepipe leather was several shades lighter than the bottom with a hand-stitched design of swirls and lines. He had never seen anything so beautiful.

"They are made in Mexico," the shopkeeper said, interrupting his thoughts. "All the charros wear them."

"Charros?"

"Mexican horsemen. They bring horses up here to sell."

"How much are these?"

"Eighteen dollars." The woman waited for a reaction.

Dalton let out a low whistle. "So, the boots that came all the way from New York are ten, but these," he said lifting the pair of tall leather boots, "are eight dollars more?" The woman nodded her head. "I tell you what. I'm going to take three shirts, one pair of pants, a new union suit and both pairs of boots, and a box of cartridges for my rifle. I'll give you thirty dollars for the lot."

The woman opened and shut her mouth a few times as if deciding what to say. Finally, she nodded slightly. "Told you we don't give credit."

Dalton pulled thirty dollars from his other pocket and handed it to her. "I'll pay you in cold hard cash. You just get those wrapped up."

He watched as the woman scurried to the counter

and put the money in the register. "Do you want these sent to wherever you are staying?"

"I'll take the union suit, a shirt and a pair of pants and those Charro boots. Everything else can be sent over to the Ranchero." The Ranchero was the finest hotel in town, which wasn't saying much since the town was in major need of rebuilding.

"I will, Mr...?"

"James. Dalton James."

The woman took a step back and her eyes darted left and right as if looking for an escape. "I've heard about you."

Dalton smiled. "Yes ma'am."

"You caught the Willis gang in Texas."

"Yes ma'am."

"I heard when you decide to go after someone, you'll bring them in dead or alive."

"Well," Dalton said, tossing peppermint sticks wrapped in wax paper on the counter. "I prefer alive over dead. The reward is greater that way."

"So, are you a bounty hunter?"

"No ma'am. I'm just usually in the right place at the right time." Dalton noticed the uneasy way that the shopkeeper was moving behind the counter. Dalton put his hands up. "I'm not going to hurt you. I just want to get some clothes and I'll be on my way." He reached in his pocket and pulled out a dime, laying it next to the candy.

The woman took the dime and laid it on the register. "I'll get these wrapped up right now."

A few moments later, Dalton was walking towards the saloon with clean clothes under his arm.

The saloon was dark and filled with men playing cards, drinking, and a few women in white peasant blouses with brightly colored skirts. Dalton worked his way through the crowd towards the bar.

The bartender was already pulling out a small glass and a bottle of whiskey. "Twenty-five cents a shot, or three dollars for the whole bottle."

Dalton raised his hand to stop the man. "Not here for a drink. I just want to get a hot bath and a meal."

The man put the bottle beneath the counter. "José!" he shouted. A medium-skinned man with hair the color of coal appeared. "Take our friend upstairs. He wants a bath."

"Si," the man said and motioned for Dalton to follow him. They walked upstairs to a room at the end of the hall. The man opened the door and motioned for Dalton to enter.

The room was dusty with peeling wallpaper and candles that were just nubs on the wall. "I'll be right back with hot water," the man said, taking Dalton's money. "You get two buckets. If you want any more, they are two cents each."

"How high do two buckets fill the tub?"

"About halfway."

Dalton rummaged through his pocket and pulled out two coins. "I'll want another bucket then."

The man nodded and disappeared down the hall. Dalton looked around at the small room. Other than the peeling wallpaper, the room was clean. A large enamel tub sat in the center of the room. A wooden chair and washstand with a looking glass above it were lined up against one wall. He spied a folding razor, scissors, and a bar of soap on a dirty lace doily next to the washbasin. In the corner stood a partition, behind which someone could undress.

Unwrapping his packages, Dalton draped his clean clothes over the folding screen and walked over to the washbasin. Looking at himself in the looking glass he grimaced. It had been months since he truly gazed on his reflection. His skin was weathered from riding in the hot sun for years chasing Frank Drummond. He looked much older than his twenty-five years.

Dropping his hat on the chair he ran his fingers through his deep brown hair. It had grown since he left home. It was now past his shoulders and in desperate need of being washed. He looked like one of the Indians he saw on his travels. Using the scissors, he trimmed his beard as close to his skin as he could, then picked up the razor, snapping it open.

He ran his finger along the blade of the straight

edge. *It was dull.* He would need to wait to get shaved. Putting the razor down he pulled the boot jack out from underneath the washstand.

It was a beat-up piece of wood with a tapered slat and a notch at the top. He stepped on the wood and put the heel of his boot in the notch, yanking it off his foot. He was shucking off his second boot when a different man appeared with two buckets of steaming water.

"I'll be back with your other bucket," the man said, pouring the hot water in the tub. "When you are done, you need to empty the water. I just bring it." He pointed to a small window behind dark curtains. "You can just throw it in the street. Just be sure to yell before you toss it out. Normally there ain't no ladies walking on this side of the street, but they have been known to get drenched a time or two."

Dalton gave a little chuckle. "I can do that. Do you have a razor strop? It doesn't look like that blade has been sharpened in a while."

The man picked up the razor and put it in his pocket. "I'll bring you a sharp one."

Dalton waited until the man left and quickly undressed, dropping his clothes on the floor. Taking the bar of soap, he climbed into the tub and watched as the dirt swirled in the water. As Dalton was washing his hair, he heard a knock on the door.

"Come on in," he said, scrubbing the dirt from his scalp. The man had returned with the third bucket of water.

"Want me to pour it over you?"

Dalton nodded and leaned forward as the hot water sliced his skin. "Thanks."

When he was done, the man dropped the bucket next to the two empty ones and pulled a razor from his pocket. "This one is sharp." He dropped the razor on the washstand and turned to leave. "Do you need anything else?"

"Yeah. See those clothes there?" Dalton pointed to the pile of dirty clothes. "Burn them."

The man nodded and picked up the clothes, wrinkling his nose as he held onto them. "Enjoy your bath."

Dalton leaned back in the tub, the hot water covering his chest. He was a tall man, but if he bent his legs enough, he could slide down to where the water hit his chin. His kneecaps were cold from being exposed to the air, so he splashed water lightly on his legs and closed his eyes.

As he closed his eyes, the image of a bruised and battered Frank Drummond appeared behind his eyes. He couldn't believe that Frank was dead. What was he supposed to do now?

He didn't want to return to Ohio, even though his mother and sister lived there. Without Richard, there wasn't any reason to go back. He and his brother were extremely close. Born eleven months apart, they could pass for twins. Richard was the older brother and was very protective of Dalton. Most nights, his brother could be found playing Faro at the saloon where Dalton worked washing glasses and serving whiskey. Richard never drank, but he was exceptionally good at cards.

If only Richard hadn't gotten into the wrong card game that night with Frank and his outlaw friends.

Dalton opened his eyes and wiped the tear that rolled down his cheek. The water was cold. There was no use getting upset about Frank Drummond. It wouldn't bring his brother back.

He honestly didn't know what he was going to do if he confronted Frank. He had never killed anyone before. He heard it changes a person … having to kill another man. Fortunately, Dalton would never have to find out now.

He ran his wet hands down his face, then shook off the excess water before he stood in the tub. Quickly drying himself he emptied the tub in the street below. He could see water racing in front of the walkways down towards the cemetery at the end of town.

Placing the empty bucket back by the tub, Dalton picked up the folding razor. As he ran his finger down the edge, the sharp blade nicked his skin. Hissing, he put his thumb in his mouth, the metallic taste of blood covering his tongue. *It would do.*

It didn't take long for him to shave and get dressed. He even used the ivory comb on the dresser to comb his hair. There was a cowlick on the side and Dalton used a bit of the grease from a jar to lay it flat.

He needed to make plans.

That would involve a notebook, a lead stick, and a newspaper. And he knew exactly where to get them. He popped a peppermint stick in his mouth and headed towards the mercantile, where he made a silent bet that the woman behind the counter would be more than happy to take his money.

CHAPTER TWO

Early March 1879, Last Chance Nebraska

"You... you... *Nincompoop!*"

Heather Barnes tried to control herself. She was in Millie Taylor's house surrounded by the women who had not yet remarried after the September blizzard claimed their husbands. Pastor Barnaby Collins insisted that the women find new husbands immediately or leave to head back to where they were originally from. He did not want to be responsible for a town filled with unmarried, albeit widowed women.

Every time she thought about it, the thought of the pastor's ultimatum made Heather's blood boil. Several of the women found new husbands by writing letters to strangers, but Heather refused to even open the envelopes that she selected from the many that arrived in November.

She had been a mail order bride, marrying a total stranger once before. She was fortunate that she had made a love match, as Jackson Barnes was the perfect man for her. Now he was gone, and she had no desire to marry another stranger just so the preacher in town could have his box checked.

Heather bit the inside of her mouth and tried to think of something intelligent to say. Instead, her words just flew from her mouth without a bit of thought. *You... nincompoop!* She heard Millie stifle a giggle.

"Mrs. Barnes!" Pastor Collins said, lifting his hand to the front of his frock in faux shock. "I can't believe you would say such a thing."

"Heather," Millie warned, placing her hand on Heather's arm, a smile cracking on her lips. Millie bit her bottom lip and tried to give Heather a stern look. Millie was her best friend and could normally calm Heather right down. They had met on the train coming west to Nebraska and were inseparable since arriving in town. Right now, not even Millie could calm the rage that was seething inside her.

"I can't believe *you*, Pastor Collins!" Heather jabbed her finger in the air at the object of her disdain. The words dripped off her tongue as if the mere act of saying his name was poison in her mouth. "I've never seen someone, so self-righteous. So indignant, so pompous! You are a ...," she barked, giving a little jump, "*nincompoop*!" She gathered her items from a chair and moved towards the door. "I will never marry someone that I don't love just because you say I have to," she called over her shoulder as she walked into the cold air. "Millie, I'll stop by this week to visit."

"Mrs. Barnes!" Pastor Collins came running out of the house, as Heather climbed into her buggy. "It has been nearly six months. You need to remarry."

Heather dropped her doctoring bag on the seat next to her and turned around to face Last Chance's only pastor. "Well, then it may be another six months before I decide to do anything." She picked up the reins and raised her eyebrow. "Are you planning on nagging me until I marry someone?"

Pastor Collins gave a half bow, twisting his hat in his hands. "I just want what's best for you, Mrs. Barnes. It doesn't do for a single woman to be living alone in this wilderness," he moved his hand around for emphasis. "And especially one with two children in her care now."

"I'm going to take that as a *yes*." Heather leaned forward towards the man. "I tell you what, Pastor Collins, you may be able to bully all the other women in this town, but you won't be bullying me. I am no *milquetoast*. I have half a mind to sell my ranch and take my butcher shop to the next town over before I let you tell me who I may or may not marry." She sat back up in the seat. "I may never marry again."

"But Mrs. Barnes…"

Heather didn't listen to anything else as she slapped the reins on the back of her horse and headed towards the dirt road leading from Millie's property. As Heather passed the fencing that separated her friend's fields from hers, she felt her chest start to burn. Taking a deep breath, she gulped air as a tear started to fall down her cheek. She tried to concentrate on the small stream weaving between the two properties.

Giving a little sob, the tears started in earnest. She pulled on the reins, stopping the buggy along the edge of the field, and placed her face in her hands.

Why did Jackson have to die?

She couldn't imagine living in Last Chance without him. She recalled his letters when they were courting over thousands of miles. She fell deeply in love with him and the area as she read his letters filled with stories about the land and people of Last Chance.

He was the butcher in town, and he kept the town safe from predators. When a mountain lion would wander too close to the herd, Jackson was sent to take care of the problem. The local ranchers paid Jackson in meat, which he would then sell at his shop, along with the furs. He also organized hunts with a Lakota Indian named Red Eagle and traded heavily with the Lakota tribes that lived on the Great Plains.

Heather thought Jackson was gentle through his communications, and when she finally came to the small western town, she realized her future husband was so much more. He was kind, always lending a hand and looking for those that needed help. Heather recalled so many times when he would deliver meat to a family in need and not expect anything in return. He always told her that because the Lord had blessed them so richly, they needed to bless others.

Her husband had a heart for people. He encouraged her in becoming a midwife and cried with her when she would return home after losing a baby.

What Heather would give to have Jackson's arms around her once more.

"Heather?" a soft voice called to her. Heather felt something grab her arm and she shrieked, opening her eyes to see Beatrice Collins standing next to the buggy. Bea quickly removed her hand. "I didn't mean to scare you."

Heather wiped the tears away from her burning cheeks. "I was just deep in my thoughts." She took several deep breaths. "What can I do for you, Beatrice?"

"I just wanted to apologize on behalf of my brother…"

Heather lifted her hand. "You don't need to do that, Bea. He is quite aware of what he is doing."

Bea twisted uncomfortably, wringing her leather gloved hands together. "I know. He means well. He just has a peculiar way of going about it."

"Well, that isn't reassuring in the least."

"Look at how many people have gotten married once more? Good matches with good men. These men provide protection and since we can't be landowners, it ensures the protection of our property as well."

Harrumph! Heather exhaled loudly. "I'd rather sell my property than to be forced to marry a man I didn't know or love."

Bea leaned back over and put her hand on Heather's arm once more. "Don't think ill of Barnaby. Please," she pleaded. "He has his faults, but underneath all that …"

Heather watched Bea struggle for words. "Awkwardness?" Heather offered.

Bea smiled. "Awkwardness is a good word. Underneath all that awkwardness is a good man. A God-fearing man."

Heather shifted in her buggy. "Do you know what I'd like, Bea?" Bea shook her head. "I'd like to see him have a taste of his own medicine. I'd like for him to be forced to marry someone he didn't love and see how it feels."

Beatrice stepped back. "Heather! You shouldn't say such things."

Heather lifted her tear-filled eyes to her friend. "I know. Jackson always said that one of these days speaking my mind would get me in trouble. I guess that day is now." The sound of buggies and people traveling down the road toward town caught her attention. She could see Pastor Collin's buggy coming down the path. "I need to get back home to Cecily and Arthur."

Beatrice moved into the grass so Heather could lead her horse on the dirt road. "What are you going to do?"

Heather shrugged. "I don't know."

"I don't want you to leave, Heather." Bea gave a small smile. "I know Millie would be lost without you."

"Millie has her new husband now. I have my new family to look after. I'll pray about it and see what I should do."

"May I stop by tomorrow?"

"I have to go see Lauren Hale. She's due in two months."

"The next day perhaps?" Bea looked hopeful.

Heather nodded. "That would be nice. Come in the late afternoon and have supper with us." She gave a light slap of the reins on the horse's backside and waved to Beatrice as they headed down the road. As she turned into her property, she ignored the Pastor's buggy riding by. As good as it felt to give the interfering pastor a piece of her mind, she was embarrassed about causing a scene in front of all the women. Those women were her friends and she didn't want any of them to think ill of her.

Once she had parked the buggy and put the horse in its stall, she walked outside and looked around. It was still cold. Even though there were signs of Spring around the corner, there was still a chill in the air.

The barnyard was empty. All their animals had been butchered to feed the town, apart from a milking cow. There were a few chickens that scratched in the hard dirt looking for bugs that were close to the surface. Cecily should have collected the eggs already.

Cecily and Arthur Poole lost their parents in the blizzard. Mr. Pool was with Jackson, Red Eagle, and the other men hunting for winter meat. Mrs. Pool was found frozen in the local park with a baby in her arms. She had tried to get to the schoolhouse to find their children, but was unsuccessful, as were many of the parents in town.

Cecily and Arthur came to live with Heather until arrangements could be made to find additional relatives that could take them in. Heather had grown very fond of the two children and considered them her family now making plans to adopt them.

Thankfully, Last Chance had an attorney! She was glad she waited. It saved her from having to ride to

Grande Platte. It wasn't a priority, but Heather wanted it done. Heather sighed. *So many things to take care of.*

She pulled her wrap tighter around her and headed towards the house; the glow from the lantern through the flour cloth curtains calling her. The curtains needed to be replaced. They were tattered and worn. *That wasn't a priority either.* When she arrived in Last Chance, Heather found Jackson's home so charming she refused to change a thing. As things started to wear, she was so busy tending mothers-to-be that she just didn't have time to get everything done.

"Mama Heather!" Cecily called as Heather pushed through the door. "You're home."

Cecily was small in stature for being eight years old. She had pale blonde hair that Heather spent hours combing knots out of, every single night. *How that child managed to tangle her hair so badly*, Heather had yet to figure out. Dark lashes surrounded large blue eyes that shone brightly against her pale skin. A small nose, rosebud lips, and two rosy cheeks that Heather just wanted to squeeze rounded out the child's features.

Arthur came running up and threw his arms around Heather's legs. "I'm glad you are back." Where his sister was blonde, six-year-old Arthur had brown hair and large brown eyes. His cheeks were red from sitting so close to the stove.

Heather handed her bag to Cecily, then knelt in front of Arthur. Kissing the boy's warm cheek, she ruffled his hair. "I'm glad I'm back too." Cecily took Heather's doctoring bag and placed it near the settee. The bag was always stored in the same location in case Heather ever had to run from the house in a hurry because someone was about to have a baby. "Have you started supper yet, Cecily?"

Cecily gave Heather a quick hug. "No. I was fixing Miss Poppet's hair."

Cecily held up the doll she kept tucked under her arm for as long as Heather had known the child. Heather gently took Miss Poppet from Cecily and examined the doll. Miss Poppet had a soft body and face with two small black button eyes. The doll was dressed in a gingham dress with a tear in the front, revealing two small, padded legs. When Heather suggested making the doll a new dress, Cecily broke down and cried, as her now-deceased mama made the dress for Miss Poppet from an old tablecloth.

"What happened to Miss Poppet?" Heather asked fingering the torn dress.

"Arthur tried to cut her hair."

"Did not," Arthur replied, crossing his arms.

"Did too," Cecily said, sticking her tongue out at her younger brother.

"We'll have none of that," Heather gently

chastised. Turning the doll over she could see a large patch of yarn hair was missing from the back of the doll's head. "Well, it appears that Arthur created a mess of this."

"You gonna punish me?"

Heather looked at the small child. "Why would I do that? You know what you did was wrong. I want you to apologize to your sister and then we are going to go to town to get some yarn. Miss Poppet needs some new hair."

"What about supper?" Arthur asked. Heather heard the boy's stomach rumble loudly.

"Why don't we go to see Miss Hollie at the diner?"

"Really?" Arthur asked, rubbing his belly.

"Really," Heather concurred. She turned the boy around and gave him a slight swat on his padded bottom. "Now go wash your face and hands and change your shirt. I need a cup of tea and then we can go." She pointed at Cecily. "You as well. I need to talk to both of you about something important."

Cecily hugged Miss Poppet closer and ran to the room she shared with Heather to get changed. Heather sighed as she took off her hat and placed it on the settee, along with her heavy wrap. She walked to the stove and placed her hands close to the side of the kettle. It was hot, which meant it would only take a few minutes to boil. Heather lifted one of the burners and placed a few sticks of kindling inside. Once the wood caught fire, she returned the burner and moved the kettle over the heat.

As she placed a cup and a tea tin on the table, she saw Arthur racing by with a wooden bucket. He slammed the door as he ran out onto the porch and then once more when he raced back inside. Water sloshed over the side of the bucket as he disappeared behind his bedroom door. Heather chuckled. Two children certainly made life interesting.

Her tea was brewing as the children came from their rooms. Cecily had on a blue calico dress with a pinafore covering the front. Arthur had changed into his church-going shirt, but he had on the same dirty pants and scuffed boots. Heather made a mental note to get the children some new clothes.

"I couldn't tie it," Cecily said, presenting her back to Heather. Arthur scrambled onto a chair and sat looking at Heather.

"Do you want some milk?" Heather asked as she tied Cecily's bow. Arthur nodded. She patted Cecily's shoulder. "Go grab the hairbrush and I'll work these knots from your hair." As Cecily ran to get the hairbrush, Heather poured two glasses of milk and handed one to Arthur. She poured her tea and added a splash of milk from the pitcher on the table.

"Here you go, Mama Heather," Cecily said, handing Heather the brush. Heather's heart clutched each time she heard the word Mama from Cecily's lips. She had always wanted children. Perhaps God provided these two angels to her since she didn't have any of her own?

Cecily sat in the chair and sipped her milk as Heather worked the brush through her tangled hair. The girl's locks were super fine and silky. Heather ran her fingers through the strands and worried a knot between her fingers. Finally, it was loose enough so she could get a brush to break through the tangled hair without hurting Cecily. Arthur sang softly to himself as he drank his milk. Heather recognized it as one of the hymns they sang in church.

"When we go to town, I need to mail a letter," Heather finally said.

Arthur stopped singing. "Are you sending for a husband?"

Heather paused detangling Cecily's hair. "Where did you hear that?"

"Everyone at school is talking about how their Mas are getting hitched. I think Pastor Collins has made everyone mad."

Heather gave a little chuckle. "Maybe." She thought about Bea's words. Even though they may not convey her feelings, they might make sense to a younger child. "Perhaps he just wants the best for everyone."

"Even us?" Cecily asked.

"I know he wants the best for you. Which is why I wrote a letter."

"To get us a new Pa?"

"No. I'm thinking of selling the ranch."

Cecily turned abruptly in the chair. The brush flew from Heather's hand and hung limply from Cecily's hair. "Are you getting rid of us?" Cecily asked, tears starting to fill her eyes.

"Oh no," Heather insisted. She placed Cecily's glass on the table and wrapped the girl in a hug. "I would never get rid of you."

"What about me?" Arthur asked.

Heather opened her arm to encourage Arthur to receive a hug. When the boy moved closer, Heather had both of her children right where she wanted them. *In her arms.* "I would never get rid of you either. In fact, I would like you to become my children permanently."

Cecily's eyes grew wide. "You'd be our mama?"

Heather nodded. "I'd like that very much."

Arthur tightened his arms around Heather. "I love you, Mama," he said.

It was the first time Heather heard him call her Mama without her name attached. She felt her throat thicken and blinked back the tears that were rapidly developing.

"I love you, too. Both of you." She pressed kisses against the tops of the children's heads. "We will go see Mr. Cairn when we get to town. I'm sure there is some paperwork we would need to fill out."

"Why do you have to sell the ranch then?" Cecily asked.

"Well," Heather started, then paused. "I was thinking that we could go on a grand adventure. My parents live in Pennsylvania and I know that they would love an opportunity to meet you."

"So, we'd move?"

Heather nodded at Arthur. "I'm sending a letter to my mother asking her to find us a home."

"I don't want to leave Last Chance," Cecily said softly.

Heather pulled her close. "Neither do I, sweetie, but I don't have a choice."

"Miss Reed says you always have a choice."

Heather snickered. Trust her best friend to plant a perfectly logical idea into the mind of a child. "Well, let's see if I get a response first." She pulled the hairbrush from Cecily's hair and gave it one final stroke before putting the brush on the table. "So, who's hungry?"

Arthur's belly rumbled in response.

"He's always hungry," Cecily laughed.

"Then let's get our coats and head to town."

CHAPTER THREE

May 1879

Dalton inhaled deeply. The scent of something delicious wafted through the air and caused his stomach to growl. Apart from an apple to tide over his hunger, he hadn't eaten since dinner the night before.

Finally, after a four-month search and nearly a month on horseback, he was crossing into a small town situated along the river.

The New Mexico marshal found a small advertisement in April's newspaper announcing a farm for sale in Last Chance, Nebraska.

The name of the town might be peculiar, but the farm sounded perfect. Dalton immediately sent a telegram to Mr. Cairn asking to purchase the property.

The farm was small enough for him to manage on

his own, came with goats, a milking cow, chickens, and a large barn. The house, per the attorney, was small, but comfortable.

Dalton was told that there was an established business associated with the property, which suited him simply fine. It meant that he would be able to make a living without having to chase bandits and outlaws.

Now, he just had to get something to eat, find a place for the night, and seek out Mr. Cairn to complete the purchase on the farm. *Last Chance wasn't the easiest town to get into*, Dalton thought. Once you arrived at the Platte River, you had to take a hand-ferry across the rocky waters. Thankfully, a few other people were crossing, so they took turns pulling the wet ropes to arrive at the other side.

The town wasn't too small, but it wasn't too large either. It would be perfect for him. He walked into the cool of the livery, leading his horse behind him.

"Hello?" he called into the darkness.

"Back here," a voice replied. "Be right out." Dalton allowed his eyes to adjust to the darkness. He could see several stalls, only a few with horses. After a few minutes, a man appeared, wiping his hands with a rag. "Howdy, stranger." He shoved the rag in his pants and stuck out his hand. "Dave McFarland. I own the livery. Can I help you?"

Dalton took his hand, shaking it a few times before

releasing it. "Dalton James. Just got to town. I need a place to keep my horse for a few days."

"James, you say?" Dave scratched his chin. "You aren't…" He waved the thought away with both hands. "Naw… never mind. You can't be him." He walked over to one of the empty stalls and pulled open the gate. "You can put him in here."

Dalton nodded. "Much obliged. Can I keep my saddle here just until I find a place to stay for the night?"

"There are saddle horses over there," Dave said, pointing into the dark corner. "And the hotel is two blocks down and on the right."

"Perfect." Dalton led his horse into the stall. There were clean straw and two buckets, one with water, the other with oats. "Shouldn't be more than a few days." He took off his saddlebags and placed them in the straw. "How much do I owe you?"

"I charge by the week." Dave named a price, accepting the bills that Dalton handed him. "Includes food and water and cleaning out the stall. I can put your horse in the pasture during the day."

"Sounds good." Dalton found a curry brush on the side of the stall and brushed down his horse while the animal munched happily on the oats and hay. When he was done, he returned the brush and carried his saddle over to the wooden horses in the corner. There were several worn saddles already there. He wondered what stories those saddles would tell about their riders if they could talk.

After securing his saddle, he picked up his bags and flung them over his shoulder. Priority one – find where that delicious smell was coming from. Dalton's stomach growled.

"Hollie's is right past the hotel. Best vittles in town."

"Much obliged," Dalton said heading back out into the sunlight. As he strolled away from the ferry depot and livery, he took a moment to peruse the town. Businesses were lined up along the river. Many were closed and several others stood empty. The post office appeared busy as did the mercantile further up the road. Keeping his eye on the mercantile, Dalton lost sight of where he was walking.

"Ooof!" a feminine voice called. "You should watch where you are going." The voice sounded angry.

Dalton looked down to see a woman in a blue dress lifting herself from the ground. "That goes both ways, ma'am." He shifted his saddlebags to the other shoulder and reached down his hand.

The woman looked at his hand and ignored it, choosing to roll herself over before standing in the middle of the road. "Look at my dress," she cried, trying to brush the dirt from the fabric.

"I'm sorry ma'am. I wasn't looking where I was going."

"That's apparent." The woman stood at her full height, which was only part of the way up Dalton's chest. At well over six feet, most women barely reached his chin. She reached up to the top of her head and adjusted the small hat that had moved during her fall. "Stuff and nonsense," she said pulling the pins out to fix her hat.

Dalton laughed. "Stuff and nonsense?"

The woman pulled out another pin and her hair came tumbling down from the chignon on the back of her head. She turned to look at him and Dalton felt his breath leave his body. His pulse quickened and he could hear a roaring in his ears.

The woman before him was the most beautiful woman he had ever seen. Her hair was the color of cornsilk as she tried hastily to pin it back in place. She missed one curl that hung down her shoulder. Dalton wanted to reach out and see if that curl would grip his finger.

Her eyes were bright blue and reminded Dalton of a summer sky. They were surrounded by thick lashes that blinked in rapid succession as she looked at him. Several freckles dotted her nose and cheeks, signifying that she was in the sun quite a bit. Her skin was still pale with two peach-colored blossoms on her cheeks, and she had a pert little nose that was flaring. It reminded Dalton of a skittish horse. He moved his eyes further down until they rested on her full lips. They were the color of inkberries. He had seen women use the berries to color their lips and cheeks, but Dalton could see that this woman used no cosmetics. Her beauty was natural.

Right now, those beautiful lips were forming an O as she stared at him. Her bright eyes rounded and then squinted as she stared at him. "I bet you are one of those men who thinks everyone should move out of the way." She jabbed her finger towards him. "Well, not me, mister. Not. Me."

Dalton tried hard to not break out into a roaring belly laugh. "You must have a bee in your bonnet to be so cantankerous." He moved aside to let her pass, watching as she put her pert nose in the air and walked past. Her skirt caught on the edge of the boardwalk and he heard the fabric tear.

"Oh bother," she said, huffing.

"One second." Dalton leaned down and removed the fabric where it was caught on a nail. "I hope you can fix that."

The woman exhaled, her nostrils flaring once more. "I know how to sew, sir. It is one of the many skills I have."

Dalton felt his cheeks lift in the corner. "I'm sure you do." He tipped his hat toward her and turned on his heel. "Have a good day, ma'am," he called over his shoulder. He heard her frustration as she swished her skirt and her boot heels thudded against the wooden boards.

His nose, and belly, led him down the next group of buildings to a large picture window. He could see several tables inside covered with checkered cloth. A blackboard in the window displayed the day's specials. There were only a few people in the diner and a woman was cleaning tables. She spied Dalton staring inside and lifted her hand in greeting.

He returned the gesture and looked at the menu.

Meatloaf.

It was one of his favorites.

He hadn't had a homecooked meal in a while, and although this was a commercial establishment, he had no doubt it was home cooking.

He walked around the side to the door and entered. A small bell rang on the door and everyone turned to look at him. Dalton took off his hat and nodded to the men sitting in the corner.

The woman with her hands filled with dishes walked towards a door in the back. "Find a table and I'll be right with you," she called over her shoulder. "Coffee?"

"Yes, ma'am." Dalton walked to the table nearest the window, set his bags on the floor and slid into the chair. He placed his hat on an empty chair and looked out the window at the people walking past. One thing he noticed was that everyone he saw walking by the window was a woman. There were no men at all.

The sound of a mug sliding across the table caught his attention. He turned to see the woman smile as she moved the enamel mug in front of him. "You must be new in town. Don't recall seeing you before."

"Just got here. You must be Hollie."

The woman's brow furrowed. "How do you know that?"

Dalton lifted the mug and took a sip of coffee. "That's good," he said putting the mug back down. "Dave at the livery told me to find the diner, ask for Hollie, and that you'd feed me well."

"Don't know how good it will be. Sometimes the cook can get grouchy."

Dalton laughed. "Hopefully today isn't one of those days."

"Fortunately for you, it isn't. You picked a perfect time. We normally get busy in two hours. What will you have?"

"I'll take the special and piece of whatever pie you have."

"Apple or apple?"

"Apple?" he asked hopefully.

"Good, because that is what the cook baked today." Dalton let go a laugh. It felt good to be around friendly people. New Mexico was nice, but they didn't take kindly to outsiders. "I'll go get your meal. Just let me know if you need a refill on your coffee."

"Thank you."

His eyes followed the swish of her skirt as she headed once more to the back of the restaurant. She stopped to fill mugs at the table with two men. He heard them ask her a question and she turned her eyes back towards him before answering. The man nodded and looked at him intently. Dalton noticed he had a star on his vest. Groaning, he cupped his hands around his mug and turned to look out the window once more.

Hollie returned a few minutes later and placed a piping hot plate in front of him. He could see the steam coming from the meatloaf and mashed potatoes. Thick gravy covered the meal. "Do you need ketchup?"

"This is fine. Thank you." He picked up his fork and dug into the meal. The meatloaf was moist, filled with onions and seasonings. The gravy was flavorful and not a lump was found. How the cook managed that he wondered. He was used to working around clumps of flour that hadn't quite blended into the sauce. The potatoes were creamy with the right amount of butter and salt.

When he was done, he scraped his fork along the bottom of the plate to get every single drop. Hollie came and refilled his coffee cup.

"Still hungry?"

"I haven't eaten much. That was the best meal I've had in a long time. I'll take a second dinner."

Hollie's eyebrows flew up in surprise. "I'll be right back then."

"Give my regards to the cook."

Hollie smiled. "You just did."

Three plates later, Dalton leaned back in the chair. He was going to sleep well tonight. His belly was full, and he'd be in a real bed, not on the hard ground. He might even pay for a bath.

"You ready for pie?" Hollie asked, filling his mug once more.

"Not yet," Dalton rubbed his belly. "Think I'll just continue to watch if you don't mind. I'll have that pie in a bit."

Hollie nodded and leaned her head towards the large window. "See anything interesting?"

"I noticed that there are a lot of women walking by, but I've only seen one or two men. Why's that?"

"You really are a stranger. Don't you know? This is Last Chance. Most of our men died in that blizzard last fall."

"I think I read something about that in the paper, but that was months ago. I didn't realize... I'm sorry ma'am. I hope you didn't lose anyone."

Hollie put the enamel pot on the table. "Nearly everyone did."

"How did it happen if you don't mind me asking?"

"We had a terrible summer, a drought killed most of the crops. The men went hunting to find food for winter." She picked up the pot once more. "Over two dozen men went out and only one returned. The blizzard was so fast that most people were stuck for days."

"I'd still think there'd be more people here."

"When the snow finally melted a few days later we realized we lost more than just the men on the hunt. Many townspeople died as well. Men, women, and even children." Hollie sighed as she looked at the wall as if trying to recall the terrible time. "A party went out to look for them. They never returned. The sheriff knew where Jackson Barnes, along with his Indian friend were going. Can't recall that name right now."

"Jackson Barnes?"

Holly nodded. "Yes. He led all the hunts around here."

"I'm purchasing the Barnes property."

Hollie dropped the pot on the table and coffee splashed on the tablecloth. She fell into the chair and lifted her hand to her blonde hair, smoothing it back. Dalton thought she looked tired. "I guess it is true then," she said softly.

"What's true?"

"Mrs. Barnes threatened to leave town. I guess it is

coming to fruition."

Dalton took a sip of his coffee. "What are you women going to do?"

"Most of the women are looking for husbands. The preacher wanted us to get remarried as quickly as possible. Several women have already found husbands because of an advertisement in the paper. I guess the town will get back to normal soon."

"Are you looking for a husband?"

Hollie laughed. "Oh heavens no. I already found one."

"He's a lucky man. His wife can cook."

"I'll be sure to tell him. I guess you need to see Mr. Cairn?"

"How did you know that?"

"Only lawyer in town right now."

"Can you tell me where I might find him?"

"One block that way," she said pointing. "You can't miss it. There is a placard outside." She stood and gathered the plates. Picking up the coffee pot she gave Dalton a little smile. "You ready for that pie now?"

"Yes ma'am."

Dalton turned to look out the window again and he spied the woman in blue, this time with two small children. The children broke free and ran towards the mercantile, disappearing behind the door. The woman slowly walked towards the door.

It gave Dalton a moment to admire her without being obvious. Her hat was still askew on top of her head and the one wayward curl was down her back now. She had a trim waist that Dalton could span with his hands. He wondered if she was married. If the women were trying to find husbands, he just might be in the market for a wife.

He watched as she turned, a man approaching her from behind. The suited man said something to her and he could see that whatever it was didn't make her happy at all. Her face contorted and she raised her hands, gesturing as she spoke. Whatever it was, it was none of his business.

"Here you go," Hollie said placing the pie on the table. "It will be fifty-five cents for everything."

Dalton pulled a bill out of his pocket and handed it to her. "Keep the change."

Hollie pocketed the money. "If you need more coffee just shout." The door jingled and more people entered the diner.

Dalton took a bite of his pie, the apples and cinnamon exploding on his tongue. He turned to look across the road, but the people were gone.

CHAPTER FOUR

"Mrs. Barnes!"

Heather turned to see who was calling her. Relief coursed through her body when she realized it was Mr. Cairn calling and not Pastor Collins.

Heather managed to avoid the pastor since the outburst at Millie's house. When Bea stopped by to ask why they weren't at church, Heather fumbled through a few excuses, but Bea knew the truth. After three Sunday's Bea didn't stop by anymore. As much as Heather loved her friend, she was quite relieved when the visits stopped.

"Mr. Cairn! How are you today?" Heather asked. "Cecily and Arthur went into the store. Walk with me?"

"Of course." Mr. Cairn kept pace with Heather as

she slowly walked down the boardwalk. "You've been very difficult to reach, Mrs. Barnes."

Heather shrugged her shoulders. "I admit I've been avoiding town. But I am always at home."

"I've stopped by not twice, but three times."

"Oh. I may have been out checking on my patients. You know several are due soon."

"Don't pay attention to such things, Mrs. Barnes."

"Well, you have my attention now. What can I do for you?"

"We have some business to discuss; but not here on the street."

Heather looked around to see who might be listening. There were several people outside the post office and down on the corner, near the ferry depot. No one appeared to be paying attention to anyone else.

"Have you heard anything about the advertisement, Mr. Cairn?"

"That is exactly what I wanted to talk to you about. I finally got a letter from a man in New Mexico who is interested in buying the property."

"That's wonderful," Heather said softly.

"What's the matter, Mrs. Barnes? I thought that it was what you wanted."

Heather turned to the man who was just a few years older than her. "I do. I did. I mean I do, but I need some time to get everything sorted and head East."

"All you need to do is put your belongings in a trunk, get a ticket and you can be on the first train out of here. The man is willing to purchase all the furnishings as well."

"Hmmm. I guess I'll have to think about it since we received an offer." Heather turned and continued walking. "Is he going to pay the asking price?"

"He paid five hundred dollars more."

Heather's eyebrows shot up. "Five hundred dollars?" Mr. Cairn nodded. "Well, he is either rich or doesn't care about money." She pretended to pick a piece of invisible lint from her jacket and then smoothed the fabric sleeve.

The blue outfit was one of her favorites. A tailored jacket that fanned out like a duck's tail in the back. Several pleats were carefully folded and sewn together. The full skirt had a bit of lace at the bottom hem. Well, it used to.

Until she ran into that cowboy.

Heather tried to put such unpleasant thoughts out of her mind. Yet, they still lingered.

The man was handsome enough. He was tall, even taller than Jackson. His brown hair was a bit long, and his beard was scruffy. Not even his chocolate brown eyes could make him appealing.

Heather sighed. She knew it was a lie. The man

was incredibly handsome. Broad shoulders, leather enrobed wool pants, long legs, and scruffy boots. He wasn't a gentleman, but there was something about him that intrigued Heather.

"Mrs. Barnes," Mr. Cairn said, interrupting her thoughts.

Heather snapped her eyes back to Mr. Cairn. "I apologize; I was lost in my thoughts."

"I said, the bank in New Mexico wired the money this morning."

"Already?"

Mr. Cairn nodded. "It appears that Mr. James wants to settle matters as quickly as possible. In fact, he is arriving in town this week."

Heather lifted her fingers to her lips. "My goodness. I guess that is good news."

If it was such good news, why did Heather feel ill to her stomach?

"I was hoping that you could stop by the office tomorrow morning and we can go over the paperwork."

"What about the adoption?"

"Well, adopting is an informal matter."

"I want to make sure that those children are truly mine before I leave town. They are my children now. Just as if I birthed them."

Mr. Cairn raised his hands. "I have no doubt, Mrs. Barnes."

"Well let's just make sure it gets done."

"Yes. Yes. I'll do everything I can."

Heather stopped walking and turned towards the attorney. "I sense hesitation in your voice."

Mr. Cairn shoved his hands in his pockets. "It would go a lot smoother if you were married."

"Married?" Heather shrieked. Several women stopped what they were doing and turned to stare. "You are worse than that… that... *preacher*!"

"Mrs. Barnes. Please."

Heather held up her hand. "I will be there tomorrow morning, Mr. Cairn. Please excuse me as I go find my children before they gobble up all of Mrs. Talley's sweets." Mrs. Talley wouldn't allow any child to leave the store without a treat from one of the large glass jars she kept on the counter.

Heather quickly moved towards the mercantile. As she opened the door, Millie and three children with sticky faces walked out.

"Look, Auntie Heather," Millie's daughter, Mary Rose, said lifting her hands. They were covered in red from the peppermint stick that was melting in her hand.

"Oh, my goodness. You are going to need a bath tonight, aren't you?"

Millie laughed. "I found your two charges in there as well." She nodded towards Arthur. "It appears that he is going to be a scoundrel! He talked Mrs. Talley into giving each of them two peppermint sticks."

Heather giggled and looked at her children. Cecily smiled widely, revealing a bright pink tongue. "Oh goodness." Arthur had a ring of colored sugar around his lips. "I think these two will need a bath as well."

"Bath night ain't until Saturday."

"Bath night is whenever I say it is, young man," Heather laughed.

"Where are you headed?" Millie asked, taking Mary Rose's sticky hand then releasing it. She flexed her fingers before wiping the sugary mess on her skirt. "Good thing tomorrow is laundry."

"Let's walk towards the park," Heather suggested.

"Good, because there is something I want to talk to you about."

Heather raised her eyebrow and glanced sideways at her friend. "I want to talk to you as well." She pointed down the road. "You children run ahead." The children took off racing towards the park. "Don't get too far ahead though," Heather called. "I still want to see you."

"We'll catch up at the schoolhouse," Millie said. "I forgot my lesson plan book."

Heather walked at a leisurely pace up the road.

"Now what do you want to talk to me about?"

"I know you've been looking to sell the farm…"

"About that," Heather interrupted.

Millie put her hand up. "Please, hear me out." Heather signaled for Millie to continue. "I know you've been looking to sell the farm. But I'm going to need you here. At least until October."

"What's happening in October?" Heather's eyes grew wide as she looked at her friend. Millie's face was slightly puffy with a green tint and she had circles underneath her eyes. She watched Millie's hand move down and cover her belly, almost subconsciously. "Oh Millie," Heather cried. She felt the burning behind her eyes and wiped at them with the back of her hand. "I will not cry," she insisted. Hugging her friend, she squealed. "You are going to have another baby!"

Millie wrapped her arms around Heather. "I need you to be here when I have the baby. I can't do this without you."

Heather released Millie and the tears were starting to fall in earnest. "Of course, I'll be here. Are you sure?"

"Well, it isn't my first child. I missed my menses," she whispered, "and then I started counting days. The sickness, not being able to be around certain scents. Why I went into the barn the other day and I thought I was going wretch right on Robert's boots."

"You've not been married even two months."

Millie laughed. "Heather, you are the midwife. You should know that babies don't have any timetable. What a wonderful gift God has brought us."

Heather was happy for her friend. She truly was, but she was sad at the same time. Sad that she and Jackson didn't have any children. Sad that Millie was going to have her second child and Heather had no prospects of remarrying. By her own choice.

She and Millie made a promise that they would raise their children together. How would that happen if she left Last Chance? She looked at her friend as Millie waved to someone in the distance.

Millie found love in the form of a man hiding in her barn. Robert "Deuce" Taylor was wanted for murder but was found innocent when the actual murderers came demanding money and confessed to everything. Heather hadn't seen her friend look this happy in a long time.

"Now, what is your news?" Millie finally asked.

Heather sobered. "It's nothing. Mr. Cairn needs to see me tomorrow."

"Oh!" Millie said looping her arm through Heather's. "Is it about the adoption?"

"Y-yes. That's it," Heather replied softly.

"You don't seem happy."

Heather gave a sharp laugh. *Isn't that just what Mr.*

Cairn said?

"The news is just so overwhelming." Heather looked around. She could see the river between the two buildings and focused on the waves moving across the water. "That's all. There is nothing wrong."

"Good," Millie said.

They walked beside a whitewashed fence surrounding the schoolyard. Heather could see the children playing inside the fencing. Bea and Barnaby Collins were outside tending to the cemetery that ran along the river. There was a small wrought iron fence surrounding the headstones.

Pastor Collins smiled and raised his hand to Millie. Millie waved in return. As his eyes moved to Heather, he dropped his arm and a scowl appeared over his face. Heather lifted her lips in the biggest grin and waved exaggeratedly to the pastor and his sister.

Through clenched teeth, she said, "You know his face is going to freeze that way."

Millie laughed. "So will yours, Heather. So will yours." They entered the schoolyard and Millie headed towards the door of the one-room building. "Are you coming in?"

The last time Heather was at the school it was the day the blizzard came. She was stuck inside the building with several students, Altar Pennington... *now Laingsburg,* and Millie for five days. They lived off soup that Altar made with meat bones Heather retrieved from the butcher and leftovers from the children's lunch pails.

"I'll wait out here while you go in." Heather gave her friend a little wave. She walked to the far end of the schoolyard. She could see the whole river if she leaned over the fence just a little. Turning, she leaned her back against the wooden fence and watched the children play tag in the yard.

Cecily and Mary Rose shrieked with delight as Arthur held out his sticky hands and chased them around the bushes.

Heather watched as Pastor Collins raked up sticks and leaves from around the gravestones. Bowing her head, she said a little prayer of repentance and asked God to soften her heart towards the clergyman. She had just said amen when the cacophony of loud voices traveled up the river.

She leaned over the wooden fence, ignoring the picket as it pressed against the underside of her ribs. *Thank goodness for whalebone corsets*, she thought. She could see a commotion on the other side of the river as several men on horses climbed aboard the ferry. Heather squinted her eyes as the yelling continued near the depot. She hoped the squinting would make her sight better. As she made out the shapes, she dropped her reticule in the mud. *It couldn't be*!

"Millie!" she yelled, leaning over to retrieve her bag. She ran towards the school building. "Millicent!"

"What is it, Mama?" Cecily said. Arthur ran into the back of her with a thud.

"Why did you stop, Cece?"

"Children, I need all of you to get into the schoolhouse immediately."

"What is it?" Cecily asked again, panic evident in her voice.

Heather placed her hand on Cecily's back and nudged her toward the school. "Please just listen to me." She grabbed Mary Rose's hand, not caring that she would soon be coated in the sticky mess. "Let's go."

Millie opened the door. "Why are you yelling, Heather?"

The sound of the yelling was getting louder through the town.

Heather shoved the children into the schoolhouse. "I need you to stay here, Millie. Don't open the door unless it is someone you know."

"What is going on, Heather?" Millie cocked her head as she listened to the words coming over the town. "Are they yelling *Indians*?"

"Who's yelling Indians?" Arthur popped his head from behind Millie's skirt. "I wanna see."

"I want you to stay here with Miss Millie, young

man. I'll be back for you shortly."

"Heather, you can't go down there."

"There is a white man with them, and it looks like he is injured."

"Oh my!" Millie said. "We'll be here." She closed the door and as soon as Heather heard the lock click, she picked up her skirt and started running back towards the end of town.

Men were starting to gather near the riverbed, many with rifles in their hands. She spied women and children running up the side streets back toward their houses. Several women remained behind the line of men, standing on tiptoes as they tried to peek out to the river.

Heather raced forward, knocking people out of the way. She was out of breath when she finally arrived at the edge of the ferry landing. "What's going on?" she yelled to Michael Darcy, Last Chance's only lawman.

"Looks like Indians are trying to cross the river." He never removed his eyes from the ferry.

"That doesn't make sense. If they were coming this way, they'd cross further downstream where the water is shallow."

The sheriff's eyes snapped to hers. "How do you know that?"

"That is where Red Hawk would cross when he visited Jackson."

"You are friends with Indians?"

Heather gave the man a pointed look. "Of course. Aren't you?"

She watched the lawman shake his head and turn back around to watch the ferry.

Heather couldn't see who was pulling the ropes. She could tell the man was white, even though he wore deerskin breeches. He didn't move with the grace of the Indians. She wished she could see what tribe it was coming across the river.

Heather moved further down the ferry landing. The Indians had dismounted from their horses apart from one, who sat proudly on the painted pony beneath him.

"Is that war paint?" one of the men asked, lifting his rifle to his shoulder.

As the party came closer Heather saw the white man lift a piece of fabric and wave it around like a flag.

"What in tarnation?" someone asked.

"It's *Makhpia Luta*!" Heather yelled. "Put your guns down. It's Red Cloud."

"Who is Red Cloud?" the sheriff asked.

"He's Red Hawk's father. Chief of the Lakota people. Their tribe lives near the hunting grounds. It must be something important for him to ride all this way."

As the ferry drew nearer, Heather bounced on her

toes, waiting for the barge to reach the shore.

She could finally see the man dressed in buckskin with fringe on the edges. His dark hair was cut short, revealing several bald spots. Perhaps this man was a slave of the Indians?

There were parts of his skin that were black, indicating frostbite. His face was red and scarred, almost as if a large animal swiped its paw across the delicate skin. He was surrounded by Indian braves dressed in matching buckskin with intricately beaded breastplates.

The Indians looked at the people along the shore and spoke to each other in guttural tones. Finally, the man on horseback gestured with the edge of his spear to one of the men. The Indian brave walked forward.

"*Makhpia Luta*, great chief of the Lakota people, comes in peace." The Indian gestured to the horses behind him. "We bring food for the friends of *Luta Cetan*. Chief Red Cloud brings horses to pay his respects."

"Respects for whom?" a voice called.

"Chief Red Cloud seeks the squaw of *Hinhan*, friend to the Lakota people."

Murmurs went through the crowd.

Heather glanced around and gave a little gasp. The cowboy from earlier was standing on the edge of the crowd, watching the entire exchange with immense interest.

The chief muttered something in short tones. Jackson had taught Heather a few words and Red Hawk laughed but humored her attempts at the Lakota language.

The sheriff moved forward. "Who is *Hinhan*?"

Heather stood up on one of the logs blocking the water from racing up into the town. "Hinhan means White Owl. It is what Red Hawk called Jackson."

"*Hinhan's* squaw has hair the color of sunlight. He told us so."

"And who is this?" Sheriff Darcy gestured to the non-native man standing on the ferry.

The scarred man moved forward. "I was on the buffalo hunt with the men from Last Chance. Chief Red Cloud's hunters saved me. They took me to their home along the Grand Platte where they nursed me back to health."

"You lived here?"

"Yes. My wife is Charity Green."

Heather nearly fainted.

There was a survivor.

CHAPTER FIVE

Dalton pushed open the door to the small attorney's office. Mr. Cairn was sitting across a large wooden desk. There were two chairs in front of the desk, and one was occupied by a woman in a dark dress.

"Excuse me," he said, backing out of the office. "I thought we had an appointment."

"We do, Mr. James," Mr. Cairn said, waving Dalton further into the office. "This is Mrs. Barnes. We had some other business before our meeting."

The woman shifted in the seat, her eyes opening wide as she recognized Dalton.

"You!" she said.

"It's me." He walked over and leaned across the desk to shake the lawyer's hand. "I didn't realize the ranch was yours."

"Yes. And the businesses too."

"Have a seat, Mr. James."

Dalton pulled the empty chair away from the desk and turned it so he could face Mrs. Barnes.

Today she was wearing a long black skirt and a black jacket with pearl buttons. Her hair was perfectly coiffed and matching pearl earrings dangled from her dainty ears. The woman before him was a far cry from the woman he ran into the previous afternoon.

"Are you still wearing mourning clothes, Mrs. Barnes?"

The woman looked at him with disdain. "I didn't have time to do laundry," she quipped.

"My apologies, ma'am."

"Mr. Cairn said that you put in an offer on the farm at well above the asking price."

Dalton scratched his chin. "I did. But we can get to that. I just had a few questions."

Mr. Cairn shuffled the papers in front of him. "I think everything will be laid out in the contract, Mr. James."

Dalton held up his hand. "I wanted to ask the woman a few things before we proceed."

Mrs. Barnes leaned back in the chair. "Ask away." She raised her hands in the air. "I'm an open book."

Dalton shook his head. "I doubt that, Mrs. Barnes."

"What do you want to know?"

"How did you know those Indians yesterday?"

"My husband spent several years with them before he started ranching. They taught him how to hunt, which in turn provided a food source for the town."

"Food source?"

"Yes. For the butcher shop. Didn't you read the advertisement?"

"I knew there was a business attached. I didn't realize it was a butcher shop." His stomach churned at the thought of being responsible for supplying meat to the town. He enjoyed a good buffalo steak as much as the next man, but to have to hunt and process the buffalo? *No, thank you.*

The woman blinked her eyes. "What did you think it was?"

"I thought it had something to do with farming," Dalton shrugged. "You know, growing hay, fixing equipment."

"Everyone does their own around here, Mr. James."

Dalton turned to the lawyer. "Is there anything that says the business must go with the property?"

"No. You can sell it if you wish."

He thought that he heard Mrs. Barnes gasp.

"That can be discussed at a different

conversation," Mr. Cairn said.

"There is a contract with the town that we provide food and protect the town."

"Protect the town?"

He watched as Mrs. Barnes smoothed her skirt. "Yes. If there is a wild animal that gets too close to the town, then Jackson would track it, and make sure it didn't return." *That didn't sound so bad.* "You can track, can't you, Mr. James?"

Mr. Cairn slapped his hand against the desk causing the petite woman to jump in her seat. "Do you know who this is?" Heather shook her head. "Why Dalton James is one of the best bounty hunters this side of the Mississippi. Tracking is no problem for him."

Dalton lifted his hand. "Let's not get carried away. Besides, that contract was with Jackson Barnes, not the property. I'm sure the town can find someone new for these positions."

"Will you at least do the job until we can find a replacement?"

"Why would it matter to you, Mrs. Barnes? I understand you are leaving the town."

He watched the woman worry her hands. "About that..." Dalton raised his eyebrow. "I was wondering if I could rent the house back for a few months?" If she had asked him to swim in the river in the middle of winter, he couldn't be more surprised. Before he could respond, she continued. "It appears I need to stay here longer than I intended."

"Why's that?"

"Some things came up." She stole a glance at the lawyer.

"What things?" Dalton demanded.

"Just things."

Dalton sighed. It appeared that he was going to get nowhere trying to discuss anything with her. He turned to Mr. Cairn. "How would something like that work out?"

"Normally the owner of the property can choose to lease any part of his land. That includes the house."

"Where would I live in the meantime?"

"There is a room on the side of the barn," Mrs. Barnes offered. "Red Hawk would stay there when he visited."

"You had Indians staying on your property?" Mr. Cairn lifted his eyebrows in surprise. "I can't imagine that."

"You saw Chief Red Cloud. The Lakota are kind people." She lifted a finger to her cheek. "Red Hawk and Jackson were... oh what is that word?" She furrowed her brow. "Blood brothers. That's it." Giving a pointed glance at Dalton she lifted her finger. "It would behoove you to have a relationship with them as well."

"So, I purchase this farm and you want me to rent you the house."

"Yes, please. It would only be for a few months until I can finish packing to head east, and I need to take care of several..."

"Things. I know." Dalton shook his head. "If I had known what was involved here, I would have kept looking for a farm." He was glad he found Last Chance. He found the town charming and the people full of life and hope. It was the perfect place to start a family and raise children. Now, it appeared that Mrs. Barnes wanted him to wait to start his dreams.

"Mrs. Barnes here is the midwife in town. Several expectant mothers will be birthing in early fall. They requested that Mrs. Barnes stay until their children are born."

"You're a midwife?"

"Yes."

"I've never met a female doc before."

"I'm not a doctor. Although I can do many of the things a doctor can do, I specialize in childbirth." She looked at Dalton once more. "Can you please help me?"

"You don't ask for much, do you, Mrs. Barnes?"

"I ask for what I need. Nothing more."

Dalton pulled the papers over towards him. *Heather Barnes.* Widow of Jackson Barnes. Her name was Heather. It was a perfect name.

Dalton scribbled his name on the papers. "I don't want you to have to leave your house just yet. I can make my home in the barn. I've slept in worst places."

"What's worse than a barn?"

"In the desert on the hot sand with insects that give no warning before they strike."

"How dreadful."

"You don't ever want to be bit by a scorpion, Mrs. Barnes."

He pushed the papers towards Heather who scrawled her signature on the papers. She had a large loopy signature. Once they were done signing the papers, Mr. Cairn collected them and glanced over them.

"Mrs. Barnes, the money will be transferred to you once I file the deed. Shouldn't be more than a day or two. I'll draft up a lease for you both to review allowing Mrs. Barnes use of the house while she remains in Last Chance."

"Thank you, Mr. Cairn." Heather stood and gathered her bag. Draping her wrap around her shoulders, Dalton saw her freeze when the lawyer said his next words.

"Remember what we talked about earlier. It would help."

Heather nodded. "It was a pleasure meeting you,

Mr. James. I hope you enjoy your new home."

"I won't until October, but I'll enjoy what I have."

Heather shifted uncomfortably. "Well then. I guess I'll see you at the farm. I need to go get my children. Good day, Mr. James. Mr. Cairn." She swooshed her skirt as she walked past Dalton to the door. As she went by, the scent of roses wafted in the air.

Dalton breathed deeply letting the floral scent fill his nostrils. It had been a long time since he had been near the scent of floral soap. His brother's wife wore rosewater behind each ear. It was a comforting smell.

Maybe this arrangement might just work.

CHAPTER SIX

Heather left the lawyer's office and held her head high as she walked down the alley. Once she was out of sight from the main road, she leaned her arm against the wall and dry heaved. How she got through the meeting she would never know.

The cowboy was buying her farm. He didn't look like someone who knew a lot about farming, but he was right. *Why should she be concerned?* It was his property now. Fumbling around in her reticule for her handkerchief, Heather pulled out a square of linen cloth and wiped her mouth. She needed to get home and prepare supper. Arthur was probably complaining to Millie that he was starving. Heather was convinced her best friend thought Arthur was never fed.

She walked to the butcher shop and using a skeleton key she went inside. The shelves were empty, but the scent of smoke lightly filled the air. There was one barrel that still had cured pork buried beneath the salt. Heather might gift that to Mr. James. She gave a little laugh. It wasn't hers to give anymore.

She opened the door to the room where Jackson would cure pork. The sweet smoky scent of sugar-cured bacon still lingered. There was a note glued to the wall. Even though Heather had read it a thousand times, she read it once more. *Be sure to check the smokers. Two-parts hardwood to one-part wet cottonwood. I love you. J.* Heather traced the words lovingly before peeling the paper from the wall. She folded it and placed it in her pocket, giving it a little pat.

Those were the final instructions Jackson gave her before he left on the hunting trip. It was her job to make sure the smoker was smoking around the clock. Little did he know that she worked from dawn to well past dusk once the blizzard passed. Since so many animals died, the meat would have been wasted if it weren't for being able to smoke it. Heather even went from farm to farm, showing the farms how to set up a smokehouse of their own.

She walked through the smoke room and unlocked the door leading into a small backyard. The buckets of cottonwood which were normally kept along the fence had long been moved. There were normally two flat wagons that Jackson used to prepare the meat for smoking. Those had been sold. The yard was bare apart from patches of grass and several dandelions giving a bit of color to the dull ground.

Heather felt her throat thicken as she wandered through the small store once more. Jackson introduced her to many of the people in town as they came through the shop. He was well respected, and the town welcomed her with open arms. Taking a deep breath, she locked the shop and put the key in her pocket with Jackson's note. She'd give the key to Mr. James the next time she saw him.

As she walked down Stagecoach Road towards the livery, she spied Charity and Nathaniel coming out of the new doctor's office. Heather bit her lip. She should probably take a moment and introduce herself to the new physician, but it wouldn't matter since she wasn't going to be around too long.

"Charity!" Heather called, lifting her skirt and hopping across the ruts in the road. "Nathaniel. How are you doing?"

Charity was a pretty girl. A little ragged in appearances but having six children could do that to a woman. Heather was pretty ragged too and she only had two. Charity's hair was a mousy brown and she had eyes to match. She wore her hair in a chignon with a little lace day cap over it. A little chubbier than most of the women in town, Heather could see the buttons strain over Charity's ample bosom. As long as her friend was happy, that was all Heather cared about.

"Doc said Nate will be right as rain soon. He just needs to rest. The nightmares will eventually go away." Charity patted her husband's arm.

"Nightmares?"

"Charity, hush. Mrs. Barnes doesn't need to know our business."

"Nate, if there is anything I can do for you. I can make a blend of tea that will help you sleep."

"Ain't necess—"

"That would be most appreciated."

"I'll stop by later this afternoon with a tin and some instructions."

"Heard you were leaving," Charity said.

"I guess good news travels fast."

"I'd hate to see you go. The town needs you. Especially with all the babies coming."

Heather lifted her reticule and pretended to rummage inside. "I'll be here until after Millie's baby is born."

"Millie's with child? That's wonderful."

"Yes. It is. Lots of babies to be born between now and then."

"Where are you going?"

"I'm going back east to see my family. I'm just waiting for Mr. Cairn to get the paperwork together so

I can officially adopt Cecily and Arthur."

"Are you glad to be leaving?"

"I think I'm relieved that I won't have Pastor Collins pestering me."

Charity placed her hand on her husband's arm. "I'm glad I don't have to remarry now." Heather saw Nate stiffen under his wife's touch. She wondered if something else happened at the Indian camp that he wasn't saying. "It is such a blessing that Nate found his way home."

"Yes, it is." Heather tried to be happy for her friend, but the ache in her heart just wouldn't subside. Why couldn't Jackson have been found and taken to the Indian camp?

Why. Why. *Why*?

She smiled at the couple. "I pray you feel better, Nathaniel. I'd like to visit with you sometime. I'd like to learn what happened." Nate nodded but didn't say anything. Heather gave Charity a little wave and headed down the road.

"He was a hero."

Heather turned around. "Excuse me?" She hurried back towards her friends.

Nate took off his hat and ran his fingers across his head, wincing as he touched skin where hair should have been. "I said that Jackson was a hero."

"What do you mean?"

"That snow came on so quickly we didn't have time to react. We couldn't see the wagon. Jackson told us to huddle close next to one of the buffalo. There wasn't enough room around the buffalo, so he took some of the men and headed towards the next kill. That was the last time I saw him. He was trying to save those men. Jackson told us everything would be alright if we just stayed together." Nate gave a sniffle. "I'm sorry, Mrs. Barnes."

"How did you survive then?"

"I hadn't been feeling well. I don't do well with butcherin'. When the snow hit, he put me right up against one of the buffalo. We had already gutted it, so he shoved me inside. The men surrounded the belly. He saved my life. It was about six days until anyone found us. By that time everyone was dead. I was near death, but an Indian scout found me. He recognized Red Hawk and took me back to the camp."

"Oh, my goodness." Heather couldn't say anything else.

"Red Hawk stayed with the first group of men. He was a fierce brave. He told us never to give up. That the Great Father in the sky would take care of us." Nate gave a little bark. "It was alright for everyone else. They met their maker. I was the last one."

"Otis arrived about four days after the blizzard. He said everyone was dead."

"Musta been the liquor," Nate mused. He pinched

the bridge of his nose and Heather could see a tear start to fall. "I wish I had died that day as well."

"Hush, Nate," Charity pleaded. "Don't say that.

Heather reached out and touched the man's arm, gently squeezing it. She was in shock that she couldn't respond emotionally. "It wasn't your fault, Nate. Jackson and Red Hawk were doing what they loved. It wasn't your fault. Was Red Cloud able to help you?"

"It took two months before I could talk. My skin was so frostbitten I lost an ear, finger, and part of my scalp." He snorted. "They gave me an Indian name as well. *Tatanka Ska*. Darn if I know what that means."

"White Buffalo. It means white buffalo."

"White Buffalo," Nate rolled the words around on his tongue. "I guess I should be honored or something."

"It means you are a member of their tribe. It is a great honor." The temperature was starting to drop, and Heather could smell the rain in the air. "You better head home. It looks like a storm is approaching." The sound of thunder could be heard in the distance. "I'll stop by with that tea." Heather gave a little wave and ran towards the livery, arriving just as fat raindrops started to fall.

"Crazy weather we are having," Dave called as she ran inside the shelter.

"Yes, it is."

"I'll get your horse ready. Get your business sorted?"

"I did, thank you." Heather didn't want to talk about anything else. After the meeting with Mr. Cairn and Mr. James and then the discussion with Nathaniel Green, her head was starting to hurt. She leaned against the doorway of the livery and watched the rain pummel the ground. Storms tended to creep up on the small town without much notice.

Thank goodness the weather in the East was more predictable. Heather was happy to be going home. She missed her family. Perhaps she might even remarry in Philadelphia.

Mr. Cairn pleaded the case that she needed to get married to push the adoption through. Heather was certain the lawyer was in cahoots with Pastor Collins. The lawyer said the adoption could still go through; it would just take longer. She had plenty of time right now. At least until October.

There wasn't a law that said she had to adopt the children before she left. She didn't want some relative showing up and tearing the children from her home. They were a family. Maybe she should consider getting married again. Heather shook off the thought. She'd wait until they were settled back in Philadelphia before they did anything.

Closing her eyes, she listened to the sound of the rain falling. It was soothing. She allowed her daydream to guide her to thoughts of a house filled with children and a husband. She tried to imagine what her future husband might look like.

Instead of a man dressed in dapper clothes, the image of Dalton James appeared behind her eyes. He was laughing at something and Heather wanted to know what it was. The scene pulled back and she could see Cecily and Arthur running around Dalton's legs. A toddler with chunky legs was chasing them. Dalton grabbed the toddler and lifted her in his arms. He turned towards Heather and pointed. She looked at the child and gasped. The child looked exactly like her.

Heather snapped her eyes open and took several breaths.

"You alright Mrs. Barnes?" Dave asked.

"I – I am. Thank you." She looked out at the rain coming down. "I hope the rain passes soon."

"Just a spring shower. It will be gone quickly. You can hear the rain easin' up."

As quickly as it started, the rain dissipated, and the sun was shining once more. Dave hitched the horse to the black buggy and Heather climbed on board. She needed to leave Last Chance. It was a matter of principle now. After her shocking behavior at Millie's house, she felt as if she had no choice.

And now her farm had been sold.

She'd be happy once she arrived back in

Philadelphia.

Why then, did she feel so miserable at the thought of leaving Last Chance?

CHAPTER SEVEN

She was avoiding him.

He rode out to the farm the day after the purchase. He wanted to see what exactly it was that he purchased. He had done a quick ride by with the lawyer, but now it was his.

JH Ranch was the most beautiful place he had ever seen. Not too large, maybe 20 acres or so. It butted up to a field of horses on one side and a small creek on the other. Heather wasn't home and the little boy who answered the door didn't know when she would return.

When Dalton asked where he might find her, the child innocently replied, "I dunno. She's avoiding someone in town."

"Arthur!" a voice called from the back and a young girl, younger than ten, came and pulled the boy inside, shutting the door in Dalton's face.

He had to admire the child's forthrightness. Dalton stayed in the hotel two more days just to give Heather some space, but he was ready to get settled. He purchased the farm, so he had a permanent place to put down roots. Not be run out of his own house by a beautiful woman.

He spent his days wandering the town, exploring the mercantile, and talking to the other men that had arrived in search of brides. It appeared that Hollie's Diner was where all the conversations took place. He stayed quiet and listened, learning about crops, horses, industry back east, and encounters with Indians on the plains. It appeared that having Red Cloud show up like he did caused some unrest with the new men in town.

It didn't appear to phase the women. Perhaps they were used to Red Hawk walking through town.

Dalton was eating breakfast when he happened to see Heather just by chance. He sat at the same table as usual where he could watch the people come and go. She came walking by the café window, her nose in the air and a leather satchel in her hand, not paying attention to anything around her.

He had to admit she was the most beautiful woman he had ever seen. If he could just get over her sassy mouth. She certainly didn't shy away from telling people what she thought. Today she wore a green day dress with a matching hat. So far, he had seen her in three different outfits. She must have a large closet to have so many clothes. Dalton looked down at his clothes. They were the same ones he wore on the trail. Granted they were dusty, but they were comfortable and got the job done. He had limited outfits, so he made do with what he had.

He lifted his shoulder and quickly sniffed his shirt, making a face as the dirt and sweat washed over him. Ugh! He would need to wash his clothes soon, otherwise, he'd be forced to purchase new ones. He didn't think he would have time to change before meeting with the lawyer this morning. Mr. Cairn told him that he drafted the lease on the property and wanted Dalton to stop by and sign the papers.

Looking out the window, he saw Heather walking into the general store. That would at least buy him a little time to finish his breakfast. After shoveling eggs and bacon into his mouth, he dropped a few coins on the table. Hollie called to him as he made his way to leave.

"Tonight's beef stew."

"Thank you, ma'am. I'm just not sure what my plans are."

He gave a wave to Hollie and headed out the door. Heather still hadn't appeared from inside the mercantile. Glancing at his pocket watch, he saw they were to meet at the lawyer's office in fifteen minutes. Maybe he would have time to change.

He returned to his hotel room and went through his clothes, sniffing them as he pulled out the few shirts he owned. Finding the one that was the least offensive, he quickly changed and headed back down to the street.

Heather was just leaving the mercantile as Dalton rounded the corner onto Main Street. He skipped over the ruts in the road, which were softening under the spring rains, and stood at the edge of the platform waiting for Heather. She was looking down and didn't see him until she went to step off the edge of the platform.

"Oh!" she cried. When she realized it was Dalton, she wrinkled her nose. "It's you."

"Yes ma'am," Dalton said pushing his hat back on his head. "'pears I'm going to be around for quite a bit."

"It's no business of mine." Heather stepped down and increased her pace as she walked away from the mercantile.

Dalton caught up with her in two strides. "It's going to be your business for the next few months."

"We can just ignore each other then."

"Was that your son at home?"

Heather stopped for a moment. "What?"

"I stopped by and a young boy answered the door. Told me you were avoiding someone in town."

Heather gave a sharp laugh. "I can't believe he said that." She continued walking.

"He's honest."

"Too honest. He has no shame about telling you anything."

"He appeared to be a sweet boy."

"He really is. Especially with everything he has been through. His sister too."

"I can't imagine them losing their father. But at least they have their mother."

Heather shook her head. "They are my children, but I didn't give birth to them."

"How's that?"

"Their parents died in the blizzard. Their father when he went on the hunt. Their mother when she took her youngest child and tried to walk to the schoolhouse to get them. We found her and the baby in the park."

"I can't imagine."

"It was terrible, Mr. James. So much loss. So much death. I don't ever want to have to worry about the weather again."

"Is that why you are leaving?"

Heather shrugged. "I'm leaving for a lot of reasons." She glanced up the road. "Oh bother."

"What?" Dalton looked in the same direction. He didn't see anything but a clergyman walking alongside a young woman.

Heather grabbed Dalton's arms and pushed him in front of her. "You have to make sure he doesn't see me."

"Why's that?"

"It's a long story. But I did something stupid and now I need to leave."

"I'm not following."

"Pride is a terrible thing, Mr. James. A terrible, terrible thing."

"I can't imagine you doing something that terrible."

"I did. I let my frustration get the best of me."

"Now, that I can imagine."

Heather moved a little closer to Dalton. She smelled of lye soap and sunshine with a hint of flowers. He closed his eyes savoring her scent. "Is he still over there?"

"Who? The preacher? He's coming this way."

Heather popped her head around Dalton so quickly she nearly lost her balance. Dalton grabbed her by the waist steadying her. Heat seared his hand and he quickly let her go. Heather's eyes flashed to his. *Interesting. She must have felt it as well.*

"Mrs. Barnes," the long-legged clergyman said running towards them. "Mrs. Barnes, I've been meaning to talk to you."

Heather gave a little cough and stood as tall as her petite height would let her. "Pastor Collins, I have been rather preoccupied. In fact, I'm on my way to a meeting right this very minute. This will have to wait."

"My dear Mrs. Barnes... is it true?" The clergyman took off his felt hat and worried it in his hands. "Are you leaving Last Chance?"

"Yes, Pastor Collins, I am. This is Mr. Dalton James. He has purchased the property. I must insist that you let me by. I need to get to my appointment."

Pastor Collins gave an exaggerated bow. "Mr. James. It is my most humble pleasure to meet you. I do hope you'll like Last Chance."

"I like what I've seen. I liked it enough to purchase a home here."

"Please know that although we have services every Sunday, the rectory is open anytime you need to find Godly counsel."

"I will try to remember that." He pushed past the preacher. "We do have to be getting to our appointment."

"I do not want you to fret, Mrs. Barnes. I have graciously forgiven you for the words you said in haste. As my own dear sister, Beatrice, told me ..." he raised his eyes heavenward, *"Barnaby she said, it is your Christian duty to do the right thing and forgive those that oppress us.*" His lips curled up in a smile that was more pain than pleasure. "I have most deeply forgiven you, Mrs. Barnes."

Heather started walking a little faster. "I am most appreciative of your sentiments, Pastor Collins, but I am already late." Dalton watched as she nearly ran around the corner and disappeared towards the attorney's office.

He looked at the pastor that was smiling sheepishly at him. "Pastor Collins, was it?"

"Yes sir. Pastor Barnaby Collins at your service." The pastor glanced down the road where Heather disappeared. "I do not know what is going on with that woman."

Dalton furrowed his brow. "That woman lost her husband."

"That is why she must remarry."

"Remarry?"

The pastor nodded. His brown hair falling in front of his eyes. "Yes. It is my calling as a man of the cloth to lead these women away from sin. They should marry as soon as possible."

Dalton furrowed his brow. "Is that why she is leaving?"

Pastor Collins stopped short. "I don't know why she is leaving. It would be best if she married…" He tilted his head and looked at Dalton. "If you purchased her house, where will she be staying?"

"In the house."

The pastor looked horrified. "With you?"

"I'm the landowner. Mrs. Barnes is renting the house until she leaves this fall."

"But where will you be staying, young man? It is extremely inappropriate for you to be there."

Dalton rubbed the back of his neck. He needed to think carefully about his next words, as he didn't want to cause Heather any more trouble. "I have a room at the hotel," he finally said.

The pastor appeared pleased with the answer. "That is fine. I do expect we will see you at church on Sunday?"

"I will make every attempt to be there." He pointed down the road. "I need to catch up with Mrs. Barnes. We have some papers to sign."

"Good. Good. I hope you enjoy your stay in Last Chance." The pastor did not attempt to move. "You aren't by chance looking for a wife, are you?"

Dalton nearly choked. "Excuse me?"

"Barnaby!" A young woman called from across the road. "You are going to be late."

"It appears I need to leave as well. I'm coming, Beatrice," he called as he ran across the road, his frock flapping behind him.

Dalton shook his head. *What an odd gentleman,* he thought. He wasn't exactly sure why Heather might be leaving town, but he'd bet a dollar that it had something to do with the pastor.

Heather sat in the chair and tried to collect her thoughts. *Oh bother,* she thought. She felt terrible about leaving Dalton alone with Pastor Collins, but she couldn't bear to be around the insufferable man.

Mr. Cairn looked at her from across the table. "Mrs. Barnes, have you thought anything more about what we talked about?"

"I've not had a moment to think about it," she lied. It consumed her every waking moment. However, she wasn't going to be rude to Mr. Cairn as he pressed her regarding marriage. *Why was marriage so important?* She had survived very well these last six months without a man. Yes, there was no reason to get married, *thank you very much.*

She heard the click of the door and turned to see Dalton come into the room. Why did he have to be so handsome? He walked to the desk and pulled the chair out the same way he did previously. He turned it slightly before sliding in. He had a perfect view of Heather. She squirmed in her seat, the scrutiny making her uncomfortable.

"I apologize," she said softly.

"For leaving me alone with the pastor?"

Heather nodded. "I just… I can't…" she lowered her head.

"Let's get this done and then we can talk."

Mr. Cairn passed a set of papers over the desk. "You are renting the house from Mr. James. The rent was removed from the purchase price of the house. Mr. James, in return, secures the barns and the land. Access to those is not included in the price of the rent."

"What about my cow?"

Mr. Cairn lifted his brow. "You mean Mr. James's cow."

"Oh. I guess that is right," she said softly. She didn't own anything anymore. She gestured to the lawyer. "Please continue."

"For renting the house there are a few stipulations."

"Stipulations?" Heather wrinkled her brow. She rubbed the bridge of her nose, willing some of the tension to leave her head.

"Yes. You agree that Mr. James may have meals with you and your family daily and that you will be responsible for doing his laundry."

Heather felt her blood boil. That was wives' work. She was most definitely not anyone's wife. "I don't think I can do that."

"Why not?"

"I might not be home every evening. What if I'm called away for a birthing?"

"Heather…," Dalton said softly.

"No." Heather lifted her hand. "I can't be responsible for one more thing. Besides, I don't even do my own laundry."

"You don't do your own laundry?" Dalton was flummoxed. "I thought all women did laundry."

Heather gave him a smug smile. "Then you have a lot to learn about women, Mr. James. I take mine to Maggie in town. She needs the money. Does mending, too. Why just yesterday I took a dress over to her to have her repair the lace at the bottom of the skirt."

She watched as Dalton leaned his head back and laughed. "How about this, Mrs. Barnes? I can't keep eating at the diner. How about I take meals with you when you are home. As for the laundry, I'm more than happy to pay for Maggie to do mine as well. You just need to arrange it."

Heather sighed. Dalton gave her a smile and a wink. *Why did he remind her of Arthur?* That small child knew exactly what to do or say to get Heather to melt. She would have to make sure that she kept her emotions in check around Mr. James. Giving a little nod, she turned to Mr. Cairn.

Mr. Cairn made some notes in the margin.

Once three copies of the lease were signed Mr.

Cairn handed a copy to Heather, one to Dalton, and placed one in a paper folder on his desk.

Heather took her papers and folded them in thirds before stuffing them in her basket. Dalton held open the door so Heather could move into the bright sunshine.

"Let me escort you home, Mrs. Barnes," he offered.

"That's not necessary."

"I'm not your enemy. You don't have to be snippy with me."

Heather looked contrite. "I apologize. That wasn't my intention. I have patients to see in town. I won't be going home until later."

Dalton nodded. "I understand. I hoped to be able to move into the barn shortly."

"How about tomorrow? I'll make sure the bedding has been washed."

"Are you taking that to Maggie?"

Heather laughed. "No. There are certain things, like bedsheets, that I will wash myself."

"I'll see you tomorrow then, Mrs. Barnes."

"Tomorrow then," Heather responded softly.

"Oh, and please call me Dalton, since we will be living close."

Heather quickly glanced around the town, making

sure no one was listening. "Don't ever say that," she said through clenched teeth. "You don't want the pastor showing up and insisting we get married."

Dalton gave her another wink. "I suppose you are correct."

"Heather!"

Both Dalton and Heather looked around to see Charity Green approaching them.

"Charity, what's wrong. Did something happen to Nate? Or one of the children?"

Charity looked frantic. "I tried to find the sheriff, but he wasn't in his office."

"Was Linda there?"

Charity shook her head. "No. No, I don't know what to do." Heather noticed the woman's hands were shaking and she was starting to sob.

"Tell me what's wrong, Charity."

"Wendy went out to the barn. One of the goats was mauled in the yard. Then she heard it."

"Heard what?"

"A screaming like the devil himself was on the earth. She came running in. I went out, but the animal had gone. I saw fresh tracks in the dirt. There was a mountain lion in the barn." Charity put her head in her hands. "It was so close to the house. What if it took one of my children? I couldn't imagine."

Heather felt her heart seize. It could have been her barn. Or her children. She moved over and rubbed Charity's back lightly. "You get home to your family. We'll take care of it."

Charity nodded and Heather watched her friend walk up the road.

"Take care of it, Heather?" Dalton rubbed his hand down his face. "How do you suppose we take care of it?"

"Come on, Dalton, let's go." Heather started walking to the livery. "I have my horse and buggy here."

"Where are we going? What about your patients?"

"I'll get to them. No one is due immediately. As for where we are going, I'm going home and you're going hunting."

CHAPTER EIGHT

"Have you seen any more tracks?"

Dalton looked at Heather. It had been three days since Charity found the mountain lion in her barn. He returned his gaze to his meal and shook his head. "No. It looked like the tracks went off to the far side of the river."

"Towards Wildcat Hill?"

"Wildcat Hill?"

Heather nodded. "Yes. There is a place Jackson talked about called Wildcat Hill. I guess it got its name from the mountain lions that live there."

"Maybe." He speared a potato and put it in his mouth, chewing thoughtfully. "I figure that it must have been a momma cat and she was looking to feed her babies. It is spring after all."

"Mama cat or not, I don't want to think of a wild cat being that close to the house." Heather ruffled Cecily's hair. "That is why I don't want you going outside."

"Dalton can shoot it. He's shot a lot of men," Arthur said around a mouthful of stew beef.

Dalton's gaze snapped to the small child. "Where did you hear that?"

"Don't talk while you're eating, Arthur. You could choke." Heather pushed a cup of milk across the table. Arthur finished chewing and took a sip of milk before answering Dalton.

"Uncle Robert says that you hunted down and found many outlaws. He says there isn't a man dead or alive that hides from you. You're fa-fa, oh what's the word?"

"Famous?" Cecily offered.

"That's it. Famous."

"Finding them and shooting them are two different things." He didn't want to have this conversation. Instead, he speared another chunk of potato and waved it in the air. "Dinner is really good, Heather."

"I'm glad you enjoyed it."

"I've not had a home-cooked meal in ages. Hollie's Diner doesn't count."

"Mama made a wild strawberry pie," Cecily said. "I helped her pick the berries."

"I hope you like it," Heather said softly.

"Isn't it early for strawberries?"

"There weren't many ripe ones to be found. It didn't help that someone was too busy putting them in his mouth and not the bucket." Heather laughed, pointing her fork at Arthur.

Arthur looked sheepish and shoved another bite of stew in his mouth, so he didn't have to speak.

Dalton laughed. "I am sure I will love it. Especially if you made it."

He could see Heather's cheeks tint under the glow of the lantern.

"Are you going to teach me how to whittle?" Cecily asked.

"You promised," Arthur chimed in. He quickly swallowed his mouthful of stew and looked at Heather. "Sorry, Mama. I forgot."

"Perhaps another night. I'm sure Dalton is extremely tired and you two need a bath."

The children started to groan. "Mind your mother," Dalton said. "I need a bath, too."

"Do you like baths?" Arthur asked. "I like swimming in the creek. Doesn't that count?"

Dalton grimaced. "There's a lot of mud in that creek. The river would be better."

Heather stood and put her plate in a bucket next to

the stove. "Don't give him any ideas."

"I'm done, Mama. Miss Poppet is full." Cecily held out her doll for Dalton to see. "This is Miss Poppet."

"She's a nice doll. What happened to her hair?"

"Arthur gave her a haircut."

"We have the yarn to fix it. I've just not gotten around to it yet." Dalton stood and carried his plate over to Heather. "You don't need to do that. Just sit and I'll get you some coffee."

"You don't have to wait on me, Heather. I appreciate you feeding me. I can earn my keep." He moved closer to her. "Dinner was delicious."

Her hair was down and curled around her shoulders. He couldn't resist touching the blonde strands. His finger gently lifted the curl and watched it as it clung tightly to his finger. His eyes never left Heather's as he fingered the curl. He could see the pulse quicken in her neck and her lips parted slightly.

She felt it too.

All he would have to do is lean down and kiss her, claiming those lips for his very own. She swallowed and lifted her chin just slightly.

"Pa kissed Mama a lot," Arthur called from the table. "He looked just like that, too."

Heather jerked away. "Dalton is not going to kiss me." She peeked over her shoulder. "Are you?"

Dalton gave her a wink. "Not today, ma'am."

"Arthur put your plate in the bucket and how about I serve some pie?"

Dalton finished his pie in four bites. "That was the best pie I think I've ever had."

"Wait until you try Mama's raisin pie."

"I've never had that."

"I made one last year. We had all this dried fruit, and I didn't have a clue what to do with it. So, I made a pie."

"You are resourceful."

Heather refilled their cups. "I guess I had to be. We didn't have supplies for a while and there was no way to get to Grand Platte. The stagecoaches didn't run for nearly three months."

"Cecily, why don't you get me the yarn and thread and let me see if I can fix Miss Poppet's hair for you."

"You don't have to…"

Dalton held up his hand. "I had to learn to fix my clothes when I was on the trail. I'm sure I can figure out how to fix a doll's hair."

Cecily ran out of the room and returned with a small sewing kit and the skein of yarn. "Can you make her hair longer?"

Dalton laid the supplies in front of him. "I'll see what I can do. You go get your bath and I should have her fixed before you go to bed." He looked up to find Heather staring at him with a peculiar look on her face.

"I – I…" she started. Shaking her head, she led the children away from the room. "Let's get your bath." Dalton watched as she carried a large Dutch oven with water to the bedroom. The sound of children laughing was silenced as Heather closed the door behind her.

He took a moment to look around the house. It was comfortable. Not the tidiest house he had ever been in, but comfortable. There were handmade blankets draped over several comfortable chairs and a rag rug covered the floor. Children's toys were scattered by one wall and a small shelf hung from the wall with several frames on it.

Dalton put the doll aside and walked over picking up one of the frames. It was a picture of a much younger Heather standing under a tree. He could tell it wasn't taken in Nebraska as the landscape in the back was different. She wore a white blouse with a black skirt and smiled shyly at the camera. Dalton put the picture down and picked up the next one. It was a picture of Heather in a wedding gown. She smiled at the camera as her hand rested on her husband's arm.

So. This was Jackson.

Jackson Barnes looked like someone Dalton would be friends with. Jackson reminded him of his brother. He placed the picture back on the shelf. The other pictures must have been relatives.

Dalton gave a light sigh and returned to the table, picking up the doll. It didn't take long to create a looped hairstyle for Miss Poppet and tack the yarn in place. He noticed that the doll's dress was torn. He would talk to Cecily and see about creating a new dress for the doll.

The door to the bedroom opened and the children ran out in their nightshirts.

"Good night, Dalton," Arthur said racing to put his small arms around the cowboy.

Dalton felt this throat thicken. *Is this what having a family felt like?* No wonder his brother couldn't wait to get home to his wife and son.

"Thank you, Dalton," Cecily said picking Miss Poppet up from the table. "She looks much better." She opened her arms to hug Dalton. As he wrapped his arms around the little girl, she placed a kiss on his cheek. "Good night. I love you." Dalton watched as she skipped off to the bedroom.

"I need to empty the tub and then I'll be right back in."

"Let me get that for you," Dalton offered. He carried the tub to the side of the porch and dumped the water in the grass. He leaned the tub against the side of the porch. "I'll take that to the barn. I wasn't kidding about wanting a bath."

"If you can wait until tomorrow night, I'll heat the

water."

"I'd like that."

"Would you like more coffee?"

Dalton looked at Heather standing at the door of the house. The light from within surrounded her like a halo, shining from her blonde hair. Her features were hidden in the shadows, but it didn't matter. Dalton had each freckle, line, and tic committed to memory. He had never felt such a longing before. The longing for a wife and a family. He had to remind himself that Heather was leaving. It wouldn't do any good to start developing feelings for her.

Or had it already happened?

"It's late," Dalton said softly. "I should go."

"Is the bed alright?"

Dalton shrugged. "Not as nice as the hotel, but it will do."

Heather gave a little laugh. "I can imagine."

"I heard talk in town about a memorial ceremony."

"Ceremony?"

"Yes. I know the Indians buried or burned most of the bodies, but I guess they want to have some sort of remembrance ceremony here."

Heather wrapped her arms around her sides. "How did you hear that?"

"There's a lot of talk at the diner... I guess the

pastor is organizing it. Someone named... Bear, Dog..."

"Wolfe?"

"That's it. He's going to make all the crosses. I guess it will take him a few weeks to get that done."

"What did they say?"

"Just that the crosses will line the side of the cemetery."

Heather put her finger to her lips and chewed on her nail. "I don't want to go."

"Why not?"

"Jackson's dead. He's not coming back. I don't need a place to go and remember him. I remember him here." She pounded on her chest. "And I don't want to go to anything at that church."

"Heather, be reasonable. Pastor Collins..."

"Is just trying to help. That is what everyone is saying. Well, he wasn't helping when he didn't allow anyone time to grieve before telling them they needed to find new husbands. He wasn't helping when he was sneaking around in barns and forcing people to marry."

"Sneaking around in barns?"

"He found Robert Taylor in Millie's barn and forced them to get married."

"Are they happy?"

"What?"

"I asked if they were happy."

Heather bit her bottom lip. "I guess so. They are inseparable. I don't know how she could marry so quickly after George died."

"You need to let go of that anger, Heather."

"You don't know anything, Dalton."

"I do. I was so consumed with my anger that I spent five years chasing someone. Five years wasted."

"What happened?"

"Found him dead in New Mexico. He had killed my brother."

Heather released a little gasp. "I'm so sorry."

Dalton shrugged. "It was a long time ago."

"Not that long."

"I witnessed him shoot my brother and I vowed revenge. It was obsessed with finding the man and making him pay."

"Why are you telling me this?"

"I was so angry I missed out on so much. I realized once my brother's murderer was dead that I didn't know what I was going to do next. That anger was eating me up like a poison."

"And so, you looked for a farm."

"I looked for a *home*."

"As interesting as all this is, I'm not prepared to let

go of my anger right now."

"Is that what this is about? You're angry because some pastor wants you to marry again?"

"I want to marry for love. Not just because some ... *nincompoop* says I have to."

"Nincompoop? Is that what you called him?"

"I admit it wasn't my finest hour, but he deserved it. And now Mr. Cairn..." she stopped talking and grabbed her skirt, kneading the fabric in her fingers.

"Mr. Cairn what?"

"It's nothing. He's helping me with a legal matter."

"Is there anything I can help with?"

"I want to adopt the children before I leave for Philadelphia. I'm trying to get the papers through, but the legal process is taking a while."

"What's stopping it?"

"I guess they don't want a widowed woman adopting two children. No matter the circumstances."

"What do they want?"

"Mr. Cairn said it would be easier if I got married."

"Then why don't you?"

"Didn't you hear anything? Pastor Collins is trying to force marriage and now Mr. Cairn says I need to get married to keep my family."

"So do it. You are going to have to release your

pride, Heather. Think of the children."

"I can't get married. I didn't answer any of the letters."

"What letters?"

"After our husbands perished, we put an advertisement in the paper seeking mail order grooms."

Dalton laughed. "That's a first."

"I was a mail-order bride. Why can't a man move west to marry a woman?"

"I don't see why he couldn't."

"I was afraid I'd never find someone like Jackson."

"You don't have to find someone like Jackson. You just have to find someone. Maybe marry for convenience. You get what you want, which is a husband so you can adopt those children. The man gets something he wants."

"But I don't want to be married."

"That's why it is called a marriage of convenience."

"Hmmm. It doesn't matter. No one is coming to marry me and therefore I must leave town."

"I think we are back to the pride issue again. Are you leaving town so you don't have to get married? Or are you leaving town because you don't want to have to see Pastor Collins after calling him a nincompoop?"

"You know nothing, Dalton."

"I know more than you think I know." He gave her a wink. "Hand me my coat?"

"Oh!" Heather said, reaching inside the door and grabbing his coat from the first hook. She walked down the steps and Dalton grabbed her hand as she handed him the jacket. He held onto her for a moment longer than necessary, allowing his thumb to gently caress the back of her hand. Her eyes snapped to his. The blue orbs turning into liquid pools as she gazed at him.

"Heather ---"

Heather suddenly put a finger to his lips and tilted her head. "Shhhh."

"What?" he said. He didn't hear anything but the chirping of birds.

Birds.

There wouldn't be any birds chattering this late at night. They would be in their nests, with their heads tucked under their wings.

"Shhh," she said again, stepping further in the darkness.

The chirping sounded louder. A chill went up Dalton's spine. Someone or something was out in the darkness.

"Heather, come back inside." He could see her hand in the light reflecting from the house. The rest of her was hidden in the night.

Suddenly a scream pierced the air.

"Heather!" Dalton yelled.

She reappeared in the light and Dalton breathed a sigh of relief.

"That's her."

"The mountain lion?"

"Yes. She's in heat."

"How can you tell that?"

"By the way she's calling. Listen."

Dalton strained his ears to hear the roar in the distance. He put his hands over his ears to silence the sound. "It sounds like a woman."

"Or a child."

The calls sounded closer. Heather turned to him. "I think it's close to Millie's."

"What do you want me to do?"

"You should probably head over there and see if you can find it."

Dalton swallowed. "In the dark? I don't know, Heather."

"What's wrong?"

"I don't think I can shoot it. Track it yes. Shoot it no."

"Why ever not?"

Dalton took a deep breath.

"I've never fired a gun before."

CHAPTER NINE

Heather shook her head in disbelief.

"You've never fired a gun?"

Dalton shook his head. "Never had a need."

"But those stories!"

"Are just stories, Heather."

"But you are famous for finding the worst outlaws."

Dalton turned away and looked back out in the darkness. "Most of the posters said *dead or alive*." He glanced back at her. "I preferred the alive part. Let the judge figure them out."

"But your brother's killer…"

"I never said I shot him. I said he was dead. You inferred I shot him."

"Oh," Heather bit her lip so hard, the metallic taste of blood filled her mouth. "How did he die?"

"Doesn't matter. He's just dead." Dalton turned back and looked at her. "People are going to believe what they want to believe. There is nothing you can do about that. I could either try to correct everyone or just let it go. I can't control what other people think of me."

"You took the job protecting this town."

Dalton laughed. "Actually, I didn't. I told you I didn't want it." He took a deep breath. "I did it for you."

"For me?"

"I have no desire to run a butcher shop. Mr. Cairn is finding a buyer for me. But I don't want anything to happen to you or the children. That is why I'm doing this."

"What were you going to do if you confronted that mountain lion?"

"Try to talk my way out of it?"

Heather giggled. "No. Really."

"Honestly? I'd probably run like hell. I was going to go visit Dave and see if he could teach me how to shoot."

"You don't need to do that."

"I need to learn somewhere. What kind of man would I be if I couldn't protect my farm?" He moved closer. "If I couldn't protect what I care about."

"You care about me?"

Dalton nodded. "And the children."

"But we are leaving."

"As you keep saying. Just make sure you are leaving for the right reasons. No one is telling you to leave. That is all on you."

"But the pastor."

"He just wants his town to be happy. Godly. Safe." Dalton titled his head. "Granted he is going about it the wrong way, but I believe his heart is in the right place."

Heather ran her palms down the front of her dress. When did her hands become so wet? "I don't know." She gestured around the yard. "I don't have anywhere to live now. You own my farm."

Dalton moved closer to her. So close that the scent of horses and leather filled her senses as he stood over her. "Heather... I –"

"Yes?" She leaned towards him, her breath quickening in her chest.

He lifted his hand, cupping her face.

Was he going to kiss her?

She wanted him to kiss her.

She closed her eyes as he lowered his face to hers, stiffening slightly as she felt his lips touch hers. It only took a moment before she melted into his embrace.

Her hands wrapped around his waist, pulling him closer.

It has been so long.

Too long since she had been touched by another.

Since she touched anyone.

Jackson.

She quickly pulled away and looked at him, tears starting to fill her eyes. "Dalton. I—" The words couldn't form on her tongue. Whatever she was going to say was quickly forgotten as several loud hisses filled the yard, followed by a scream that sent chills up Heather's spine.

"Get inside. Now," Dalton demanded, pushing Heather through the front door. She quickly ran to the bedroom and grabbed Jackson's double-barrel shotgun. Searching through Jackson's wardrobe, she found a box of shells then returned to the kitchen. Dalton was standing in the doorway looking out into the darkness.

"Do you see anything?"

Dalton shook his head. "No. It appears to be coming from the east side of the farm." Heather laid the shotgun and shells on the table. "Are you going to shoot that?"

"Jackson taught me to handle a gun. I never had a use for one when I lived in Philadelphia." She quickly glanced up at him. He was watching her intently. "I'll teach you how to shoot."

"Heather." He moved into the room, closing the door behind him. "I don't think we should go out there tonight. I couldn't hit the broadside of a barn."

"I agree, but we are going to have to find her. A mother lion with kittens can be very territorial. It doesn't matter if you are an animal or a man. They can take down an entire cow. Jackson said he saw an Indian that had been attacked for getting near a litter of cubs."

"I wonder if that is what happened to Mr. Green?"

"Nate?" Heather picked up the coffee pot and swirled it around. "The markings suggest that, but it could have been a bear or another wild creature." She lifted the pot in Dalton's direction. "I'm going to make a fresh pot. This one is nearly empty." She headed towards the door, whistling as she walked.

"My mother taught me women shouldn't whistle."

Heather turned on her heel. "I'm sure your mother didn't have a mountain lioness on her property. The whistling lets her know I'm here and to stay away."

"I'll have to remember that."

Heather went on the porch but kept the door open so she could see Dalton. He picked up the rifle and caressed it with his large hand. The large hands that were holding her just a moment before.

Heather felt a heat rise in her body. She

remembered this feeling. It was the same attraction she had to Jackson. Fortunately, she and Jackson were married. Dalton was certainly not her husband.

She needed to focus on the task at hand, and not what it would be like to forget who and where she was. *No matter how tempting.*

After rinsing the pot and dumping the wet grounds off the side of the porch, Heather refilled the pot with cool water and carried it back inside. She added coffee grounds and several clean eggshells and put the enamel pot over the burner.

"I've never seen anything like this before."

"Jackson got it in trade. It's a Parker." She picked up one of the shells and handed it to him. "Inside this cartridge are many small pellets. They scatter when the shot is fired. This one," she said, handing him a longer shell, "is filled with rock and dirt. You use this when you don't want to kill whatever you are shooting at, but you want to inflict quite a bit of damage."

Dalton rolled the shells in his hand. "You can feel the difference in the weight."

"Yes. I saw you had a six-shooter when you were in town."

"It's empty."

"You carry around an empty gun?"

"I told you, I don't know how to fire it and I didn't want to risk shooting myself in the leg. I've seen it happen."

"You are either the craziest or the bravest man I've ever met."

"It is rather intimidating." Dalton laughed. He had a deep timbre that made Heather shiver.

"Yes, it is."

"The only gun I've seen was the one we had over the bar back home in Bellbrook."

Heather picked up another shell and rotated it in her hand. "Where is that?"

"Ohio."

"What were you doing in a saloon in Ohio?"

"I worked there. It was my first job. My father was an accountant in town. I didn't grow up on a farm, but I idolized the cowboys that came into town. I got a job at the saloon washing glasses. Eventually, I was serving beer and listening to the stories of life on the range." He stared in the distance as if reliving the memory. "My brother, Richard, stopped by every night after his children were in bed to come to play faro. He was good at it too. Never cheated. But the people he was playing with that night didn't take kindly to losing. They shot him down in the street right in front of me." Dalton rubbed his eye. "The sheriff didn't want to go after Frank. Appears Frank Drummond took delight in killing lawmen. His reputation preceded him."

"Which is why you never correct the perception about you."

Dalton nodded. "No need. If a man has a reputation people stay out their way."

"Coffee should be done." Heather moved to the stove and filled two mugs from the large pot. Handing one to Dalton she sat back down at the table and held her mug with both hands. Blowing on the hot coffee she took a sip and allowed it to warm her.

The bedroom door creaked open, and the sound of little feet could be heard coming to the main room. "Mama?"

Heather held out her arms and Arthur climbed into her lap. "What is it, sweetheart?"

"I got scared. There is a loud noise outside."

Heather rocked her son back and forth, rubbing his back. "It's just a mountain lion. She's looking for her mate."

"Her mate?"

"Her husband. She's trying to find her husband."

"Oh." Arthur yawned and snuggled under Heather's arm. "I'm sleepy."

"Where's your sister," Dalton asked.

"She was too afraid to come out."

The roar of the mountain lion was heard in the cabin once more. That was all it took for Cecily to run from the room, Miss Poppet in tow, and throw herself into Dalton's arms. The little girl hid her face in Dalton's neck. Dalton only hesitated for a moment before wrapping the little girl in his embrace and shifting her, so she sat comfortably on his lap.

"Shhhh," Dalton soothed Cecily. "It will be alright. She'll be gone by morning."

"What are you going to do?"

"Once the sunlight comes up, we'll find where she is and make sure she never comes back."

"Promise?"

"I promise."

Heather watched as Dalton kissed Cecily's hair and put her back on the ground. "Why don't you go back to bed?" he told her.

"I'm still scared."

"I wanna sleep out here," Arthur said.

Cecily jumped up and down. "Can we, Mama?"

"I suppose so. Just this once."

"I'll show you how to create a bedroll. We used them all the time when we had to sleep on the hard ground."

The children ran back to their room and pulled their blankets from the bed, dragging them to the area near the woodstove. Giggles filled the house as Dalton got down on the floor and showed them how to make their blankets into a bed by folding them in half. Heather tucked pillows underneath their heads and gave each a kiss.

"Now go to sleep. We'll be right here," Dalton said ruffing the children's hair.

Heather smiled. *We'll be right here.*

It was almost as if they were a family.

But they weren't. And they might not be unless Heather could figure out a solution to how she could adopt the children.

"I think that's it," Dalton said, sliding back into the wooden chair at the table.

"They are going to be sore in the morning."

Dalton stretched his arms. "It isn't that bad. Once you get used to your bones popping." Heather giggled. "You should do that more often."

"Do what?"

"Laugh. Your whole face lights up." Color exploded on Heather's cheeks as she looked away. "Look at me, Heather." Her blue eyes snapped to his. "You are the most beautiful woman I've ever seen. You should smile more."

"I've not had much to smile about."

"I understand. How about I help you?"

"How?"

"You mentioned earlier that you needed a husband to adopt the children."

Heather wrinkled her nose. "Yes."

"Marry me."

"You?"

"Yes. I can see that you care for the children a great deal. By marrying me you can adopt them, and I am guaranteed that I won't be a prospect for Pastor Collins' matchmaking."

"You know I'm leaving in the fall."

Dalton smiled. "That gives me several months to change your mind."

"Thank you for the offer."

Dalton tried to hide his disappointment. "Think about it. You don't have to answer now."

Heather nodded. "Tomorrow we'll set up some bottles at the end of the fence and I'll show you how to shoot."

"Do you think the cat will come back?"

"Eventually. But when it does, we will be ready." Heather yawned. "I should get to bed. You need to sleep as well."

"Are you going to sleep out here with the children?"

Heather nodded. "I'll get my blankets. That way they aren't scared when they wake up."

"I should probably head to the barn."

"Do you need me to escort you?" Heather laughed.

"I'm sure I'll be fine. If you find me in the field, bury me under that big oak." Dalton pushed away from the table and picked up his hat. Putting it on his head, he headed to the door. "Good night, Heather."

"Good night, Dalton." Heather stood and followed Dalton to the porch.

He leaned down and kissed her cheek. "I'll see you in the morning."

As Dalton's boot hit the packed dirt, another scream rang through the yard. This time it was accompanied by a lower growl causing Dalton to jump back on the porch. "Do you have an extra blanket? I'm not walking out there in the dark."

Heather nodded and walked towards her bedroom.

Dalton latched the door and took off his coat, hanging it on the peg next to his hat.

Heather returned a few minutes later with two quilts over her arm. She handed one to Dalton. "Jackson's mother made this when we got married. This one," she said smoothing the quilt on her arm, "is the one I brought from Philadelphia."

He took the quilt and laid it on the floor, folding it so it made both a bottom and top cover. Heather mimicked his movements and did the same with hers. Shucking off his boots with his heels, he put them next to the door.

"Do you want me to blow out the lamp?" Heather stared at the floor. Dalton turned to see what she was looking at. "Do you want me to move those?" he said pointing to the boots.

"N – no," she said softly. "That is where Jackson kept his boots. It has been too long." She walked over to the table and blew out the light plunging them into darkness. Dalton could hear her shuffle across the floor and crawl under her quilt.

Dalton laid on the floor and stretched out. The floor wasn't comfortable at all. He moved his arms and his legs trying to relax.

"Are you alright?" The whisper carried over the children.

"Just trying to get comfortable." He rolled on his side facing Heather, the two children tucked between them. Arthur was gently snoring. Dalton tried not to laugh. He reached out his arm over the children and used it as a pillow.

Just as he was closing his eyes he felt the touch of Heather's hand. "My apologies," she said, yanking it back in the darkness.

"You need to stretch too?"

"I figured it would be easier to put my arm this way."

"You can stretch out. I don't mind."

He felt her hand on the floor next to his.

Hesitating for just a minute he took her hand weaving their fingers together above the children.

"I'm scared."

"Of what?" he asked.

"I don't want to fall in love again," Heather whispered across the children.

"Too late," Dalton whispered back. He squeezed her hand and closed his eyes, falling into a dream of the family right before him.

Chapter Ten

"You need to move a little to the left."

Dalton adjusted his rifle aligning the jar to the barrel of the gun. It was hard to concentrate with Heather so close to him. Two weeks had passed, and he felt at home on the farm.

They didn't speak of that evening in front of the fire, and Heather had yet to answer him about his marriage proposal, but something changed between them. Heather laughed more. Arthur followed Dalton around the farm, pointing out when he did a task incorrectly. In the evenings, Cecily would climb on his lap with Miss Poppet as he read Bible stories before the children went to bed.

Every night he'd kiss Heather on the forehead and head out to sleep in the barn alone. Every morning she would spend an hour with him teaching him how to shoot before she went to see her patients. He wasn't particularly good at it, but at least his aim was improving.

If his goal was to hit the broadside of the barn.

The mountain lion hadn't returned and no one in town reported the screams or missing livestock. Dalton knew, however, that it was just a matter of time before the lioness returned. This time with hungry kittens.

He talked to Heather and they made a decision not to kill the animal, but instead, fill its hide with rocks and sand. It would hurt enough to teach the animal not to come around town, but not cause any damage. They were going to have to learn to live with the animals, and Indians, in the territory.

Dalton pulled back on the hammer and closing his eye, he breathed out, just as Heather had taught him. Pulling the trigger, he tried not to recoil from the gunstock hitting his shoulder.

"Did I hit it?" he asked.

"You closed your eyes again, didn't you?"

Dalton opened his closed eye and looked. The jar was still standing on top of the tree stump.

"How did you know?"

"Because when you close your eye, you instinctively jerk up the rifle."

Dalton handed the gun to Heather. "Maybe you

should demonstrate?"

Heather placed the gun up against her shoulder and moved it to line up with the bottle. Her face wrinkled as she leaned into the side of the gun.

"You want to hold it like this."

Dalton put his arms around her, pulling her tight against his chest. The gun was still on her shoulder and since she was so petite, he couldn't line it up with his. He placed his large hand over hers on the forearm of the rifle. The other he wrapped around her waist.

"Have I told you today how beautiful you are?"

Heather glanced up at him. "Are you trying to distract me?"

"Is it working?" He pressed a kiss against her head.

"This is serious," Heather said.

"I know."

Heather fired the gun and the glass bottle shattered, pieces flying away from the stump. She turned in his arms and placed the rifle in his hand. "You need to reload this."

"Yes ma'am." Dalton released her and walked to where the cartridges were lined up on the fence. He flipped open the barrels and placed two cartridges in the gun. Snapping it shut, he walked back over to where Heather was standing.

"I think I know what we need to do."

"What's that?"

"Millie said that she uses a reward system during the day at school. When children complete all their assignments, they get to pick a sweet from a bag she keeps in her desk."

Dalton tilted his head. "I do like peppermint sticks," he said.

"I'll be sure to pick some up when I go to town."

"Are you going to the memorial tomorrow?"

Heather shifted, swaying from side to side. "I want to, but I don't. Does that make sense?"

Dalton put the butt of the gun on top of his boot. "I know. But I'll be there to support you."

"I'll go, but only if you are there."

He looked at her. He loved this woman. Since the moment he met her, she'd burrowed her way under his skin. "I will be." Dalton threw the gun in the air and caught it with his hand. "We should probably practice some more."

"Alright. Remember what I showed you."

Dalton lifted the rifle to his shoulder and put his head against the stock so he could see down where the two barrels joined together. "I have a better idea."

"Better than peppermint sticks?"

"Yes. For every jar I hit, I get a kiss."

He lifted his head and looked at Heather. "That just

might work. Dalton?" she said softly putting her hand on his arm."

"Yes?"

"I think we should get married."

"Are you sure?"

"Yes. That way we can adopt the children."

"But then you'll be leaving."

Heather shook her head. "No. Last Chance is my home. It is our home. I want to be a family. Here with you."

Dalton contained his emotion. He wanted nothing better than to jump and yell. With his free hand, he grabbed hers, wrapping it in his warmth. "What about the people in town? You said you had to leave. You didn't have a choice."

"Those are just stories. I can't control what they say about me."

He gave her a wink. "Good girl."

"I'll speak to Pastor Collins after the memorial ceremony and apologize for my behavior."

"I think that is a fine idea, Heather."

"One more thing, Dalton." He raised his eyebrow. "I'll give you two kisses."

Laughter rang across the pasture. "Yes ma'am." He lifted the rifle back up to his shoulder and aimed.

Pulling the trigger, pellets flew, and the jar

exploded. He let out a whoop. Putting the gun on the ground, he pulled the woman he loved in his arms. "I'll take those kisses now, Heather Barnes."

"Soon to be James," she replied as she pulled him down to receive his reward.

September 1879

Dalton knelt before the wooden cross and traced his fingers across the letters that were carved in the wood. Wolfe Laingsburg had done a beautiful job on the crosses that were lined in rows along the edge of the cemetery. There would be a prayer service in the park in two weeks on the first anniversary of the blizzard that killed so many men. *But right now, Dalton just wanted to be alone.* Heather stopped by to check on Millie and then she and the children would soon join him.

Standing, he took off his hat and worried the brown felt between his fingers. "I... Uhm... I don't know what to say." He pushed his fingers through his hair and pointed at the cross with his hat. "I'm sorry that this happened to you. I know Heather misses you a great deal. But as terrible as it sounds, I'm glad I was able to get to know her. That wouldn't have happened..." he gestured around the cemetery. "Well, you know."

Shifting from foot to foot, Dalton's gaze traveled down the row of crosses. There were so many of them.

The sound of the waves lapping against the shore soothed his nerves. He could see the ferry on the other side of the river. It was calm and peaceful underneath the trees. Dalton turned back to the marker.

"I just want to tell you, Jackson, Heather knows I'm not here to replace you. You won't be forgotten. I love her just as much as you did." He scratched his chin as a smile broke out. "She told me we are going to have a baby. Due sometime in the spring. I'd like to name that child after you. I think Jackson James has a nice ring to it, don't you?" Dalton knelt once more in front of the memorial. "If it's a girl, we'll figure that out then. I'll take care of Heather. I promise you. And those kids too. We are a family now. I'd like to come to visit from time to time. Just to talk if that is alright." The sound of a bird carried over the cemetery as if Jackson were responding. "She tells me stories about you. I hope I'm half the husband that you were."

Dalton patted the cross and recited a quick prayer; a verse he had memorized since childhood. With a soft *amen,* he stood and looked around the cemetery to find his wife and children.

Heather was coming across the park with a bouquet of small purple and pink flowers in her hand. The children carried the same flowers as well as several long lilies. Dalton recognized them as the flowers that grew along the creek that ran between the two properties. He chuckled as he spied the bottom of Cecily's skirt caked in mud. Arthur had mud on his shirt from where he wiped his hands.

Life would never be dull with those children around.

His wife never mentioned his shortcoming to anyone in town and Dalton simply ignored the stories of his accomplishments on the prairie. Heather practiced marksmanship with him every evening and now a gun felt comfortable in his hand. He still vowed never to shoot another human being, but now he could protect his family if needed.

Heather spied him and waved. He lifted his hand in greeting and walked towards them, meeting them halfway. Lifting his hands, he cupped Heather's chin and gently pressed his lips to hers. When he broke the kiss, her eyes were closed, and he could hear her softly sigh. Her lashes fluttered as she opened her eyes and smiled.

"I love you," she whispered.

Dalton pulled her close. "I love you, wife. More than you could ever know."

"Did you have a good talk?" she asked softly.

Dalton grinned. "Yes ma'am. I did."

"I'm glad."

"How is Millie?"

"She can barely move. I think it will be another two weeks at least."

"That's good." Dalton slipped his hand against Heather's belly, curling his fingers around the child inside her. "How's this little one?"

"Swimming around in there."

Dalton kissed his wife's nose.

"Pa kissed Mama a whole bunch," Arthur volunteered.

Dalton laughed and grabbed the boy's hand. "And I'll be kissing your new mama even more." He gave Heather a wink as they headed towards the last cross.

"Hello, Jackson," Heather said softly. "I don't know what Dalton told you, but I wanted to let you know that we will be alright. Everything will be alright."

Dalton put his arm around Heather's shoulders and pulled her close, kissing the top of her head. He was so blessed she was his wife. He couldn't be prouder of any woman in town. She could be tough as nails or gentle as a newborn calf when it was needed.

The pastor kept a wide berth from her now that he knew she was married. It appeared that was all Pastor Collins wanted... *for the women in town to be safe and loved*. Dalton warmed to the pastor, despite the disdain many of the townsfolk exhibited. Dalton was one of the pastor's biggest champions. After all, the crazy idea matched him to Heather. He couldn't imagine a more perfect life.

"You ready to go?" he asked softly.

Heather nodded, placing a handful of Sedum below Jackson's name. He watched her wipe the tears away as Cecily and Arthur did the same.

"Can we go see Mama now?" Cecily asked. She had several wild lilies that were starting to wilt, held tightly in her grip.

"Of course," Heather said, looking over her shoulder at Jackson's cross one last time. Placing her hand on Cecily's shoulders, she led the children to the cross embossed with the name of their mother. Cecily handed Arthur one of the lilies and dropped the other at the foot of the cross.

"I miss you, Mama," Cecily said.

"Me too," Arthur replied, adding his flowers to his sister's. "We have a new family now."

Cecily nodded. "Mama Heather is our mother now. And Pa Dalton is our new Pa. You'd like them."

"They kiss a lot." Heather laughed at Arthur's declaration. "I hope you get to see all the angels and Jesus."

"I love and miss you, Mama."

"Me too," Arthur whispered.

Dalton had an urge to pick up both children and hug them tightly.

"We gotta go, but we'll come back and see you soon," Cecily promised. She turned and put her head on Dalton's belly and wrapped her arms around his waist. He rubbed her back as she cried. "Promise me, you'll never leave," she said.

Dalton lifted her chin and brushed the hair from

her eyes. "I promise, Cecily James. I will never leave any of you." He gave Heather a wink as she wiped the tears from her own eyes. "Now what say we go make this official? I understand Mr. Cairn has the judge waiting. We just need to sign the papers and then we are a forever family."

"Then we are going to get supper?" Dalton heard Arthur's stomach rumble as he asked. The boy was growing and had a voracious appetite.

"Yes, son, we are going to get supper." Dalton was taking them to the diner where he ate when he first arrived in town.

"I hope Miss Hollie has meatloaf."

"I hope she has meatloaf, too." Dalton took Arthur's hand as Heather grabbed Cecily's. Leading his family back to the main portion of town, he never would have imagined that an advertisement made in haste could lead to the family he always wanted.

LEAVE A REVIEW

The End

If you enjoyed this story! I would appreciate it if you enjoyed this story, you leave a review, as it helps readers find books from authors they love.

<u>Tap here to leave a review.</u>

<u>Join the CSR newsletter here.</u>

<u>Tap here to see all of Christine's books.</u>

<u>Click here to join the Chat, Sip & Read Readers Community.</u>

The story continues in the next Blizzard Bride's story!

A GROOM FOR JENNA (BLIZZARD BRIDES #14)

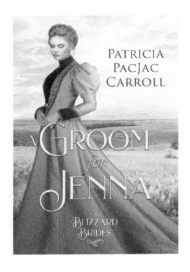

Jenna is tied to the earth, to nurture her farm, and see things grow. Alex has a wandering skip in his step and longs to see what is over the next hill. Is love strong enough to uproot Jenna? Or will it tie Alex to Jenna and her farm?

Grab your copy of A Groom for Jenna now!

Want to find out if Pastor Collins gets his comeuppance? *Find out in A Groom for Fancy.*

A GROOM FOR FANCY (BLIZZARD BRIDES #32)

A preacher's daughter that has lost everything but her faith; a preacher trying to atone for the sins of the past and a forced marriage that can be the answer to both of their prayers.

Preorder A Groom for Fancy on Amazon.

THE BLIZZARD BRIDE AUTHORS

- Christine Sterling
- Cat Cahill
- Heather Blanton
- Laura Ashwood
- Lynn Donovan
- Marianne Spitzer
- Marie Higgins
- Marisa Masterson
- Marlene Bierworth
- Parker J. Cole
- Patricia Carroll

www.theblizzardbrides.com

READ ALL OF CHRISTINE'S BOOKS

The Chapmans Series:
1. Owen
2. Oliver
3. Caleb
4. Everett
5. Alice
6. First Christmas at Flat River

The Hartman Series:
1. Annamae
2. Baxter
3. Rexford
4. Whitney
5. Verna
6. Angie

The Blizzard Bride Series:
1. The Blizzard Brides
2. A Groom for Millie
3. A Groom for Heather
4. A Groom for Lauren
5. A Groom for Charity
6. A Groom for Fancy

Agate Bay, Minnesota:
1. Gretchen's Dilemma
2. Ava's Longing
3. Nettie's Destiny

Nomad, Montana Series:
1. The Gift of Hope
2. The Gift of Faith
3. The Gift of a Wife

The Black Hills Brides Books:
1. Her Secret Past
2. Her Secret Baby
3. Her Secret Shame
4. Her Secret Love

The Christmas Books:
1. A Cozy Mitten Christmas
2. A Cowboy for Christmas
3. A Mother for Christmas

Read Christine's Other Books:
1. Gwyneth (Widows of Wildcat Ridge)
2. Moving from Maryland (Pioneer Brides of Rattlesnake Ridge)
3. Dancing to the Altar (Holliday Islands Resort #2)

<u>www.christinesterling.com</u>

ABOUT CHRISTINE

Christine Sterling independently published her first book in 2017. She writes sweet and wholesome historical western novels, as well as sweet contemporary romance novels. She lives in Pennsylvania with her husband, a spoiled Shih Tzu, two German Shepherds and an energetic Border Collie, that keep her on her toes.

She spends her time writing, thinking about writing, and dreaming about writing. Her favorite things are a good cup of tea, puppy snuggles, a movie that will make you cry and hearing from her readers.

If you like this book, please take a few minutes to leave a review now! Christine appreciates it and you may help a reader find their next favorite book!

www.chatsipandread.com

Made in the USA
Las Vegas, NV
16 July 2021